AN ENCHANTED HEART

ALSO BY JULIA V. ASHLEY

SHORT STORY COLLECTION
Jazz by Faelight

FAIRIE MARKET MYSTERIES
A Charmed Moon
An Enchanted Heart

JULIA V. ASHLEY

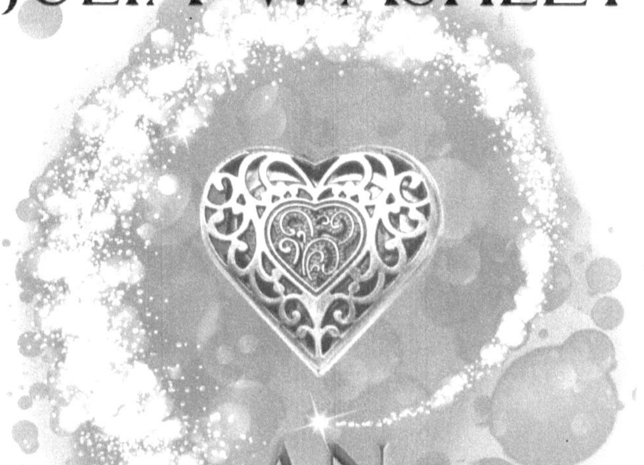

AN ENCHANTED HEART

A FAERIE MARKET MYSTERY

BOOK TWO

The story, all names, characters, and incidents portrayed in this production are fictitious. No identification with actual persons (living or deceased), places, buildings, and products is intended or should be inferred.

AN ENCHANTED HEART

To Zoë & Sam
My two imperious crows

Chapter 1

SABINE

Warmth leached from stone crypts as shadows stretched thin across the mourners' walkway. Corpse dust floated on the breeze, whirling around the homes of the dead. And wraiths shook out their creaky bones in the waning sunlight.

In answer, a gang of surly crows muttered, their sleek forms silhouetted against the deepening blue of the sky. They'd staked out a crypt for their turf. Some shifted places to more defensive positions as Sabine passed. Others held firm.

Out of habit, Sabine scanned to see if she recognized any of them, but he wasn't there. The cocky crow who'd haunted her through three murders had abandoned her. She hadn't seen him in months and had given up asking if his kin knew where he went.

He wasn't the first to desert her.

Her aunt and mother were both gone as well. Sabine used to venture through the cemetery to see if perhaps their ghosts had taken up residence. A naïve hope persisted that they waited for her to pass so that they might impart some wisdom, a dream that lingered far too long. If they were ghosts, they wouldn't be here. Her aunt would either haunt the house where she was murdered, or drift as a specter over the bayou where she'd grown up. Sabine's mother would be watching over her father, making sure he didn't wander off in pursuit of his deceased wife.

Neither her aunt nor her mother was around to help her leash her meager magic.

It didn't matter.

Sabine didn't have enough to bother with. She could transform into a fox despite being a witch, instead of a shifter. And she had a couple of other minor tricks. Mildly useful, but hardly spectacular.

The handful of werewolves she'd met while in New Orleans accused her of stealing her animal form. They'd become quite adamant about her infraction as they tied her up and dosed her with Fairy Dust. She'd escaped with the help of Detective Jean-Luc Thibodeaux, an almost friend who was no longer speaking to her. And that mite-ridden crow, her aunt's familiar before she passed.

Crooaa, one of the hooligan crows of the cemetery called after her.

Crooaa. Croaa. Croaa, the rest agreed.

"Yeah, I know. Back at you." Sabine had no time for their conspiracies. She was debating whether to continue sulking around the mausoleums or to head for the French Quarter early to liberate a croissant from an outdoor café. It was a tossup at this point.

A Creole woman with dusky skin and a knowing smile stepped from between two of the above ground crypts the New Orleans cemeteries were known for. She wore slim leather pants and a burgundy over-bust corset, so dark and shiny it gleamed like an oil slick. A heart charm hung from a delicate chain around her slender neck. Lean muscles lined her slender arms.

Metallic lacquered nails, sharp enough to serve as weaponry, tipped her slender fingers.

Sabine took a step back and wrapped an arm protectively around her worn satchel.

"What do you hope to find among the dead, *ma petite sorcière*?" the curious woman asked. She gave Sabine a lazy Southern smile, but her eyes were hungry.

"If I wanted to speak to the dead, I'd go to the Tremé and ask a Voodoo priestess," Sabine said, with the condescension born of ignorance.

"*Ma chérie, tu parles comme un enfant.*" The woman tutted at Sabine who tried her best to unwind the Haitian-French.

"Did you say I party like a baby?"

The woman peeled with laughter, her hand covering her mouth. The pewter nails came dangerously close to puncturing her eye. "You speak as a child. Do not speak to the priestesses with your *stupidité*. Now, tell Mlle. Georgette, what is troubling you?"

Sabine skirted around the woman without answering.

Nothing was wrong with her. The days were cooler. Well, at least every other day was cool-ish, you know, for the Gulf Coast. The city was filling with tourists for the parades leading up to the big Mardi Gras blowout. All easy pickings. And she finally had a friend in town, or at least a roommate, who was happy to let Sabine pay half the rent.

What did this woman think could be troubling Sabine? She didn't know her.

Sabine left the woman to her divinations, only to be stopped by a flurry of crows. Swatting them away, her hand struck something warm and wet. Repelled, she asked, "What're they doing?"

The murder of ink dipped crows settled on the ground in front of Sabine, blocking the cemetery's gate. Some threw their heads back, swallowing strips of what looked like fresh meat. Others turned their heads to and fro dodging the theft attempts of younger crows.

"Where did they get meat in the middle of the cemetery?" Sabine asked, as one crow successfully ripped a strip out of another's beak. The ruddy flesh had a flap of what looked alarmingly like skin. "Is that?"

"Shoo. Shoo, *ma corneille*." Mlle. Georgette walked into the flock, flapping her hands to break up the gruesome orgy. "Excuse the children. Tell Mlle. Georgette what you need?"

"I have to get to work," Sabine said. Which wasn't strictly true, since Sabine had never had a legit job. But it was true enough for the illegitimate job of petty thievery, which she performed like a pro.

The woman tapped one of those savage nails against her bottom lip. "You need a teacher. I see that now. And Georgette shall provide *les instructions nécessaires pour le bébé sorcière*."

Sabine squinted to better translate. "You think you're going to teach me the necessities for a . . . baby witch?"

Mlle. Georgette tutted. "So sad to be left *ignorante*."

That one, Sabine could decipher with her eyes wide open. "I am *not* ignorant." Or a baby witch, Sabine added to herself.

"Irritable," Mlle. Georgette shook her head. "It shall cost you, but it must be done."

Sabine walked around her in a wide arc. As the waning light shifted on the strange woman's torso, it glistened as if the fabric were damp—with blood.

Sabine picked up her pace, unsure if she'd just come upon the aftermath of a murder. A human one, in addition to the crow variety.

A streetcar made the turn on Canal Boulevard to head back toward the river. Sabine sprinted for it. Running in fox form would have been faster, but there were too many witnesses. She glanced over her shoulder to see the diminishing figure of the peculiar Georgette.

"You shall return, baby witch. And I will be waiting for you," Georgette called before bursting into a cloud of crows that cawed farewell.

Unnerved, Sabine hopped onto the streetcar. Without thinking, she reached into her pocket for the metal disks she used to fool the transit system.

The driver gave her the eye.

Fine.

She pulled out the exact change from her opposite pocket, then slumped on one of the wooden benches at the back. She stared, unseeing, out the window past the street to her aunt's house. Blocks of shops, houses, and churches crouched behind a row of crooked oaks, hoping tourists would pass them by on their way to elsewhere.

"Don't hide too well or no one will find you." Sabine spoke from experience.

The streetcar screeched to a stop. People hopped up and jumped off the car. Others dragged themselves on board. The car pulled away with a couple scrambling on board at the last minute. They chose to sit in front of Sabine.

Annoyed at their proximity, Sabine didn't notice the crow streaking through an open window until its wing clipped her nose. The assaulting fowl fluttered to a landing on the bench across from her.

Cr-r-ruck, it muttered, which made no more sense than any other crow talk. It twisted its head to aim a beady eye at her.

"Do I know you?" she asked. The couple turned as a duo to give her the eye. "I don't think they see you," she hissed at the bird.

It bobbed its head and paced back and forth along the bench. She didn't know if it was trying to communicate, "Yes, you know me." Or "No, they're too blind to see me." Or "You got any spare food?"

It looked familiar. But all crows did.

Sabine couldn't tell if this was her crow, or rather her aunt's crow, or just a crow crow. Maybe one of those carnivores from the cemetery hoping for a handout for dessert. If it followed her home, she'd get Meg to take a look at it. See if she could tell any difference.

Her roommate didn't have an ounce of magic in her bones, but she seemed to be drawn to those who did, like a mosquito to naked flesh.

It didn't matter. The crow abandoned her at the next stop, and Meg wasn't at the apartment. Good thing Sabine preferred being on her own.

Or so she told herself.

Chapter 2

MEGAN

Tourists crowded the shop, squeezing past one another down narrow aisles past racks of incense and poppets and T-shirts with clever witchy sayings such as "GO SAGE YOURSELF." A cool damp breeze found its way through the doors propped open to the sidewalk, a relief from the persistent heat that had lasted through December.

"Oops." A young man with a double Mohawk reminiscent of Wolverine and a questionable tattoo tittered after dropping a bath bomb on the floor. It broke into chunks, scattering its glittery guts across the floor. His friend, with a rather lovely lotus tattoo on their shoulder, crouched to clean it up.

"Leave it," Meg hollered. "I'll get it in a bit."

With a gold charm bracelet clattering at her wrist, Meg refolded T-shirts that she'd folded twice already that afternoon. People pulled them from the shelves, laughed at them, then threw them on top of an ever-growing pile for her to sort through. They pawed relics, sniffed bath bombs, and peered into crystal balls, oblivious that someone would have to follow behind and clean up their mess. Meg didn't mind. Too much.

Folding shirts and organizing rows of tarot cards helped reorder her scattered mind. Two months had passed since Valdi, her once best friend and roommate, had deserted her, leaving Meg with the full rent.

While Valdi frolicked with the Fae, examining them as if they were a rare and hidden culture, only recently discovered, Meg had weathered the grief of her former roommate's parents. They believed her to be dead, brutally murdered, and that was fine by Valdi, who didn't seem particularly concerned about her parents and didn't plan on returning to the human world anytime soon, anyway.

Turns out, the Fae weren't rare in the Big Easy. And their culture was hardly worth studying, in Meg's opinion. It involved the sport of antagonizing, sometimes maliciously, the human citizens of New Orleans. Better to avoid them like a sharp-toothed plague. The Fae carried Meg's closest friend away while she'd thanked them for the privilege.

Other than the psychic who gave readings on Tuesdays and Thursdays in the back corner, no otherworldly creatures visited the witch's shop. Meg liked the lack of mystery, content to fold shirts, restock crystal bins, and answer sincere questions about the tarot with dubious answers.

A woman with no visible tattoos or piercings plopped an assorted pile of merchandise on the counter: a faux Voodoo doll on a key chain dressed as a doctor, a crystal necklace, and a sage scented candle.

"Can I interest you in an essential oil to go with the candle?" Meg asked, as per her training.

"This'll do. Thanks." The woman beamed but wouldn't make eye contact, as if she were making an illicit purchase. Far be it from Meg to dissuade her from this harmless deception.

"Cash or card?"

The woman handed her a card and dared a glance up. "Is the owner really a witch?"

"One of the best," Meg said, even though she didn't know if the owner was a *real witch* or not. She didn't want to know.

Ignorance meant sanity.

A goblin, a for real gnarly goblin, gifted her the charm bracelet she wore. It enabled her to see the supernatural creepers so she could steer clear of them.

Working in the Sassy Witch was a boon she hadn't expected. "Real" creatures, except the aforementioned psychic and witch, avoided the kitsch magic charms. The glitzy touristy trinkets meant the owner was probably not a real witch, but Meg found her to be a remarkably savvy business woman. So, if kitsch sold, then she sold it.

Meg considered introducing Sabine to the owner. Maybe her new roommate could learn to use magic for something more than making the occasional electric fuse blow out or turning into a mischievous fox. Truth was, however, Meg didn't want Sabine to learn. With the minimal tricks her roommate possessed, Meg could pretend she didn't have a *creature* in her home.

If witches were creatures. Meg hadn't asked Sabine or her boss if they were. Not wanting to offend or be turned into a toad, if witches did such things for real.

The store grew dark as the winter sun ducked behind a cloud as if to avoid the spectacle entering. Meg looked up from the poly-mix jet black T-shirt with the bright white letters saying "WHAT'S UP WITCHES" and saw him. A tall figure with an icy gaze and a sharp smile. The Sassy Witch's clientèle parted, allowing this inhuman male to pass freely.

So much for avoiding creatures.

Meg searched around for a place to hide. A secret door, not a large demand for a magic shop. A manikin to impersonate, though she lacked the pointy hat to pull it off. Or an empty cardboard box in which to hide, but she was a size super-tall and the closest boxes were only big enough to fit a head. They originally contained crystal balls. So, she was left standing, mouth agape, a chill running down her spine as the Fae approached with a smirk of recognition on his face.

The crescent moon charm dangling from her bracelet held a vision of the night she'd met this Fae at the elusive Midnight Jazz Club. Once she'd relived the memory, she couldn't expunge the graphic scene from her brain. Some nights, she welcomed the reminder. Other times, like here in a shop full of strangers, she definitely did not need to be reminded of the vivid details of how those hands and that mouth had roamed her body.

"Good morning, Lovely," said the Fae, so pale that his skin had the barest tinge of blue.

"Afternoon," Meg muttered. She chose to behave, as if she'd grown into a more confident version of herself than she'd been last fall.

"In this stifling world, I am sure it is afternoon. But who would base their reality in a New Orleans where the noxious odor of humanity fills the air?"

"Me. I would very much like to base my reality here, and for you to go back wherever you find it to be morning at this hour." Meg continued folding shirts even though it made her nervous to take her eyes off him. This male Fae might not be the cause of her friend disappearing into the In Between, but he did tie Meg to the night it happened.

"Are these on sale?" a teenager with a creative array of piercings held up a pack of tarot that had been mis-shelved on the 50% off rack. The Fae scowled, and the teenager shrank back from the counter without ever looking at him. A bewildered and distressed look over took her.

"Never mind. I'll put it back." She shoved her way through those laughing and posing with T-shirts and crystal necklaces in the mirror and darted out the door.

Meg groaned. "You can't just come in here and scare buyers away."

"It would seem I can. Very easily in fact."

"What I meant was 'Don't'." Meg tried a fierce glare, but the Fae was taller than her, a feat most humans couldn't achieve, and she felt like a child staring up at a grownup. He probably thought she was.

"You need not bother with these vermin. I have come to escort you to the In Between."

"First, I *am* one of these vermin of which you speak. Second, my friend *disappeared* in the In Between and has yet to return. And third, *why*? Why did you come all the way here through the 'noxious odor' to ask *me*?"

The Fae leaned over the counter.

"First, no you are not. Second, I did not ask." The ice in his blue eyes made them appear as if they were polished crystals. He ran a chilled finger down her jawline, and ice arced down her neck. Her body hummed in remembrance of the touch.

His breath chilled her lips as he said, "And third, because you fascinate me."

And that was that.

Meg found herself walking out of the shop. Door left wide open. Register left unattended. Line of shoppers calling after her.

A small but persistent voice, perhaps her conscious or the shrill voice of good sense, screamed for her to stop.

Meg left it behind as well. All she took with her was the golden charm bracelet. She jangled it on her wrist, assuring herself that she would remember this tomorrow.

The Fae gave her a sharp smile. "I see you haven't forgotten."

"Nope." Thanks to the gnarly goblin vendor from the Fairie Market. The chain also allowed her to collect memories of her time with the Fae. She supposed she owed him for that, too.

A chill ran down her spine, so cold that it ached, and this time it had not come from the icy man leading her willingly into foolishness.

Behind her, tourists screeched, caught by the wards on the door as they tried to leave with armloads of unpaid for merchandise. The Sassy Witch's entry sparked with blue arcs of ethereal electricity. Its clientèle wailed. But magic was harmless, mostly. Or so Meg had been told. If they dropped their loot, the shock would stop.

But they held on.

Bad choice, Meg thought, and then made one of her own.

Chapter 3

THIBODEAUX

Outside, police cruisers gathered in the dark at the foot of the Canal Street Line. Their blue lights pulsed, out of sync with one another, as they strobed across officers corralling witnesses under the metal and glass awning. Inside, the lamplight shone through the windows into the warm glow of the streetcar. The sun had yet to get out of bed on this chilly winter morning.

If only Detective Jean-Luc Thibodeaux could be so lucky.

He swung the flashlight's harsh white beam around the car. At the far end, the reversible bench turned backwards, so the last passenger faced away from the driver and the rest of the car. The young male lounged with one arm thrown over the back of the bench, his gold wristwatch flashing in the reflected light as Jean-Luc approached.

Instinctively, Jean-Luc ran his thumb over the silver pocket watch kept in his pocket like a talisman, and circled to face the man.

Dark hair fell across the victim's eyes. The left half of his face was caught in a smirk while the other had just begun to register surprise. It hadn't quite made a decision before it froze in place.

Murder created the perfect snapshot of horror.

The victim's olive-green corduroy shirt gaped, revealing a hole in his chest. Cracked ribs protruded around the cavity that had once held a heart.

"When did he enter the car?" Detective Jean-Luc asked the driver.

"Told the lady, I don't know. I see 'em get on. See they pay, then let 'em go. I can't keep 'em all in my head. It's a long night." The driver scratched nervously at his warm brown chin.

"You talked to Officer Carmichael," Jean-Luc indicated the female officer outside, questioning the passenger who found the corpse. The man nodded, a jerky motion. He shuffled from one foot to the other, adjusting his clothes. Jean-Luc took down his name and address, although he insisted he'd given that to Carmichael as well. "Thank you, sir. I'll let you go for now. Go home and get some sleep. If you remember anything else, call the station."

The driver nodded aggressively and tugged at his pants.

"Lady said so, too. Said ask for her." He shuffled off, muttering as he went. "I got to be on my route come morning. Don't feel good about none of it. Been hearing things around town."

Carmichael had been first on the scene and started the questioning while Jean-Luc dragged himself out of bed after a call from the station around 2:30 a.m. He'd always found her to be conscientious and thorough, that is until last October when she handled a case without him while he was missing from duty.

Dark shadows swirled across Jean-Luc's vision, clouding the view of the victim's split expression. He pocketed his notepad and dug the balls of his hands into his eye sockets. It didn't help. It never did. Blinking made it worse.

Jean-Luc clenched his eyes and leaned his head back. The mists continued to drift, appearing as a fiery smoke behind his eyelids. It was not the first time the dark mists had blinded him.

It would pass, he prayed.

The first time had come only a week after he escaped the confines of an apartment of a missing person. Jean-Luc had been the lead investigator. When black mists had trapped him, the sunlight barely filtered through the windows into his prison.

At the time, he'd feared breathing the blackened air. Feared it would coat his lungs with pitch. It seemed it took root instead and began to grow. Jean-Luc could feel it. Something dark lived inside him. And on days like this, he could see it.

Opening his eyes, he looked through the mists at the garish scene before him. The victim's face flickered as the shadows swirled. The young man's mouth stretched into a scream. Flickered. His head thrown back in a silent, maniacal laugh. Flicker. He smirked up at Jean-Luc as if he had a secret.

Flicker.

Scream.

Laugh.

Smirk.

"Jean-Luc," Carmichael said, coming up the steps of the streetcar.

Luckily, his back was to her so that she couldn't see his expression. His vision cleared enough for him to focus on the gaping wound in the man's chest once again.

"Carmichael."

The sleepy sun peered over the buildings bordering Canal Street to take a peek at the gathering of police vehicles.

Carmichael stopped at his side, close enough for her shoulder to brush his biceps.

"I finished questioning the last two passengers. Forensics crew is ready to start when they get your go ahead."

A final tendril of darkness passed before his eyes. The victim leaned forward, hand held out in invitation. His eyes, expectant. And just as quickly, it was gone.

"Are you okay, Jean-Luc?" Carmichael asked. He must have tensed in the split second that the vision came and went. Her face was pinched in an exaggerated show of concern. Or at least he thought the expression looked off. Just like the victim's look of adoration. Too staged. A performance. That or the shadows were making him paranoid.

Nevertheless, he responded, "Jean-Luc."

"Sir?"

"I go by Thibodeaux at work. Professional courtesy, Carmichael."

The pensive look flickered into consternation, then it settled into a businesslike mask. "Of course, sir."

"I'll send tech in and see you at the office in the morning." Jean-Luc waited at the stairs. It took a minute for Carmichael to realize he expected her to leave with him. She caught up, and he let her exit ahead of him.

"Carmichael," his tone brought her to a stop. "Harris, on night duty, he called me from the office to report the incident." She looked confused at this abrupt change of subject. "Who called you?" he asked.

She ducked her head, hiding her face in the shadow of the streetcar, but not before Jean-Luc saw that he'd startled her.

"I, uh, must've been Harris. Yeah. Yeah, it was Harris," she said and made a beeline for her car before he could ask any more questions. They both knew Harris wouldn't call Carmichael, the assistant on the case, before calling Thibodeaux, the detective in charge.

Automatically, Jean-Luc ran a thumb over the silver watch in his pocket. Realizing what he'd done, he snatched his hand out and waved the med techs into the car.

Around the end of the streetcar route, New Orleans awoke weary-eyed. The Big Easy was always a late sleeper, but the lights of the cop cars had lured a smattering of curious spectators, mostly shopkeepers and vagrants, woken by the commotion.

To give himself time to think, Jean-Luc took a circuitous route to the precinct, past a row of shotgun houses in tight order down one side of the street and two-story townhouses down the other. A few locals biked past on their way to work. Others returned home from coffee shops with steaming beverages and paper bags oily enough that they probably held croissants.

The increased frequency of those damned mists clouding his vision had Jean-Luc worried. That, and Carmichael's dodgy answers. The fact that she made sure she was at the scene of the crime before he even knew about it. Her questioning witnesses and potential suspects before he arrived.

All that, on top of the public chaos, this would create right around Mardi Gras. They wouldn't be able to keep it quiet for long. Too many witnesses. It would be in on the morning news for sure. Maybe national news. Sensational deaths were too much for the slavering press to pass up.

No peace for the dead, or their families. But maybe shining a public spotlight on it would help turn up some info. Someone who saw something. That or it could send everyone involved to ground.

Jean-Luc was only half paying attention when a woman stepped out into the street directly in front of his car. He slammed on the brakes.

The unusually tall, slim woman appeared off balance. She swayed and caught herself, hands flat on the hood of his car. Confused, she squinted to get a good look past the glare of the windshield.

He knew that face.

The woman swayed, stood upright, and stumbled into traffic once more. Luckily, the oncoming car was far enough away to stop before running her over.

Jean-Luc jumped from his car, calling her name. "Armand!"

She swiveled towards him and nearly lost her balance again. Jean-Luc held up a hand to the man in the car as he circled around him. He approached her, hands held up. "Megan Armand? It's Detective Thibodeaux. Can I approach?"

Armand made a bobble motion with her head, which might have been a yes. So, he came to her side, wrapped an arm around her, and guided her to his passenger door.

"I'm going to take you home. Is that okay?" He didn't like the idea of her wandering the streets alone in this condition, even with the sun up.

Another head bobble. Once he got her inside and out of traffic, he waved for the other car to go on and got in the driver's seat.

"Megan, look at me." He slowly reached up and checked her pupils. They were blown, but not dangerously so.

"Have you been out drinking?" He suspected she'd done more than that.

"I know you," she slurred. "I've been to the club again."

He took a deep breath, suspecting he knew which club she meant. "The Midnight Jazz Club?"

"Yeth," she lisped. "He said 'I fascinate him.' Me." She pointed to herself. "You can check the charm."

"No need. I'm going to take you home now." Her eyes seemed to be clearing up, and Jean-Luc didn't think a hospital could handle whatever she might've consumed at the enigmatic club. "Do you live in the same place?"

"Yesss, pretty sad, huh?"

Yeah, but who was he to judge? Likely, she hadn't been able to break the lease. He put it into gear and took her to the cottage with a large oak tree in the back and an attic apartment on top. Where the alleged murder of Megan Armand's roommate had taken place.

Officially, the unsolved case was an ongoing investigation. Unofficially, Jean-Luc knew it would never be solved. Not by the NOPD.

Chapter 4

MEGAN

Meg stumbled up the stairs to the attic apartment she shared with a petite pickpocket. Already the memories of the night were dissipating like fog off the river. She repeated snippets to herself as she grabbed for the handrail in an effort to keep from tumbling back down the long single flight. Wisps escaped through her mental fingers, singeing her like steam from a kettle.

The handrail rocked alarmingly under her grasp. She let go for fear of jerking the rickety thing from the wall and fell to her hands and knees on the treads. Detective Thibodeaux helped her to her feet. He'd insisted on walking her to her door, like an old-timey gentleman.

Well, one thing was for sure, she must have been drinking, or smoking, or something. What was it the Fae did? Could they even get drunk or high?

Toppling to a seat on the landing outside her door, Meg searched her purse while Thibodeaux patiently waited a few steps below.

"You can go on, you know," she shooed him off.

"I'll see you in first, then I'll go."

See, just like one of them old timers.

No amount of digging produced the keys. So, she started emptying items from the bag one at a time. She finally had the keys in her grasp when the door swung open.

"Where have you been?" Sabine loomed over her. Which was a novel experience since the woman could barely see over the edge of five feet while Meg loomed over six. Well, she would if she weren't sitting on the steps with the guts of her purse arrayed around her.

She stuffed it all back inside. "You did that on purpose, didn't you?" Meg could hear the slur in her voice but chose to ignore it and proceed with the accusation. "You waited on the other side of the door until you knew I had the keys in my hand, then you come out here and . . . And start . . ."

"Yeah. Yeah. Laying in wait. That's exactly what I did with my morning. Now, crawl your sorry ass in here. I made you some coffee. Have a cup, then take a bottle of water to bed with you and sleep it off."

Thibodeaux helped Meg to her feet, then stepped back, ready to leave.

"Jean-Luc?" Sabine asked, as if she couldn't see that was exactly who he was.

"Just helping Ms. Armand home. I found her stumbling into the street by the market." They shared a look while Meg wavered on her feet. She slipped past them and into the living room of the tiny apartment.

"You're living here now?" he asked Sabine, which was an equally stupid question. Obviously she did, Meg thought as the couch slithered to the side when she tried to grab for it. She stumbled, tumbled over the arm, and landed, miraculously, in an upright position.

"Yeah, somebody's got to look out for her," Sabine said, as if she were the adult around here, which was ludicrous. Meg burped something unpleasant up.

"You said something about coffee?" Meg hollered louder than she'd meant to. "I sure could use some right about now." That didn't come out any quieter. Oh well.

The two of them muttered formal goodbyes, and the door shut. Meg blinked, and when her eyes opened, Sabine held a large steaming mug and a piece of toast.

"Here, this'll soak up whatever you put down last night." Sabine handed it over and sat across from her in the armchair, reclaimed from a random curbside, curling her legs up beneath her.

"Why so formal with Ol'Thibodeaux?" Meg said around a mouthful of toast.

Instead of answering, Sabine cocked an eyebrow. "You want to tell me where that puffy red streak down your neck came from? I'd assume it was a hickey if it didn't look so much like frostbite."

Meg clapped a hand to her neck. It was tender to the touch. She very nearly recollected the face of the creature who'd put it there, but it slipped away before she could grab hold of it. She ran through a list of improbable excuses she could give the foxy woman looking disdainfully over her latte.

She rejected them all, and asked instead, "You're friends, right? With Thibodeaux. He's prickly, sure, but last fall, he came when you called. He watched out for you. And you . . . Well, I don't suppose you did much to deserve it, really, but he was there for you. For us. And now you two are all polite talk and standoffish."

"We were always polite," Sabine snapped in her usual, not so polite manner. "And *I* helped *him*. He wouldn't have solved any number of cases without my help."

"How many? And no, you weren't polite. I was there, remember?"

"How many what?"

"How many innumerable cases did you miraculously help him solve?" Meg could tell she had Sabine's ruff up now, and she quite enjoyed it.

Sabine held up one finger, two fingers, and mouthed the numbers as she silently counted off cases. Her eyes scrunched with the effort, and she turned her fingers on Meg as if sighting a gun. Meg jerked as a zap struck her elbow and slid down the side of her arm. Coffee sloshed into her lap.

"What was that for?" Meg sopped up the coffee from her fashionably shredded jeans with the tail end of her T-shirt. Sabine had zapped her before with her meager magic. It didn't particularly hurt, but it was annoying.

"Just experimenting. Why is it magic slides off of you? It always does."

"Because you're not very good at being a witch," Meg said, then regretted it. It was a low blow. Sabine was touchy about her lack of training, but that was no excuse to go around zapping her friends, or her friend, singular. Meg wasn't sure if Sabine had another, other than maybe Thibodeaux, but it didn't sound like they were on very friendly terms at the moment.

The refrain from "Witchy Woman" blared on Meg's phone. She'd set it as the ringtone for the Sassy Witch shop. It seemed particularly insensitive after her latest comment. Setting her coffee aside, Meg dumped her purse on the chest that substituted for a coffee table. The phone tumbled out, nearly falling off the far side.

Sabine swiped it up and answered the call. "Mlle. Armand's answering service. Make your message short if you want me to remember it."

Meg rolled her eyes, which set the couch to swerving again. She grabbed hold of the arm to steady herself while Sabine listened extended response on the other end. Sabine smirked, and the air around her hands crackled. Always a dangerous sign.

"Sabine, what're you up to?"

Instead of answering, her roommate flipped her hand waving away Meg's concerns as she said, "Mlle. Armand was called away on an unexpected trip."

True enough, Meg thought.

"She's having difficulties returning."

Also true. Her head was reeling, and her stomach churned.

"I will be filling in during her absence."

N-O, Meg mouthed.

"No," Sabine repeated out loud. "No bother at all. The shop will be opening on time. I'll come in early to be sure the merchandise has been inventoried, and the shop put to order. Mlle. Armand appreciates your concern." Sabine tapped the off icon and gave Meg a sly smile.

Meg shot out of her seat, or she tried to, banging her knee on the chest and falling back as a sharp pain shot through her calf. Moaning, she clutched her leg, but still managed to eke out, "No, Sabine. You are not taking over the shop."

"Why ever not?" Sabine said innocently as she located her auburn slippers and put them on her tiny feet, snatched the keys from the doorknob where Meg must have left them.

Meg turned and hung over the back of the couch. "Because you are a thief. I cannot allow you in the shop unsupervised, or even supervised. Fox in the henhouse, and all."

Sabine pulled her auburn hair into a sloppy bun. "This fox is quite adept at taking care of henhouses, I assure you."

Meg pushed herself up and lunged for Sabine, who adeptly sidestepped. The room spun, and Meg sat hard on the back of the couch. Thank God they got a new one, or she'd be on the floor several times over by now.

"I'll be fine by opening. I just had one-to-many hurricanes last night. A quick nap's all I need."

"You," Sabine pointed an accusatory finger at her, "Have been consorting with the Fae again. You don't think I know about the last time? And the time before that? What I don't know is how you keep slipping out of their grasp."

Meg opened her mouth to contradict, but her lack of memory didn't help. She thrust her arm out. "Only the once. Check the memory charms if you don't believe me."

The smirk slipped from Sabine's sharp face. "Meg, where's your bracelet?"

The gold chain gifted to her by the gnarled goblin was missing, along with the attached charms. Each one carried a memory from the Fae she interacted with. All gone, and the memories, too.

Meg had no way of tracking what had happened to her or it once she left the shop.

Who would steal it? And why? It couldn't be for any good reason.

Sabine's mouth formed a perfect 'O,' which Meg assumed was short for 'Oh Shit!'

Chapter 5

SABINE

The Sassy Witch's door stood wide open. Merchandise piled thigh high, forming a levee against vagrants passing in the night. Outside the door, a Creole man leaned against one of the cast iron columns supporting the balcony above. He scratched at the graying stubble on his sun aged skin, pulled a filter less cigarette from his mouth, and tipped his hat to Sabine as she approached.

"Good of you to show up right early. Miss Beauchamp'll be waiting on me. Don't want the coffee to get cold or that youngin to eat all the pastries afore I get there. Would we?" The man tipped his hat again and strolled off down the street.

Sabine had absolutely no idea what he'd just said, but she nodded back as if she did, or as if it didn't matter. It looked as if he was guarding the doorway. Surely not. He disappeared around the corner, and she climbed over the mound of goods at the door.

A familiar car drove past as Sabine dragged the merchandise aside and closed the door. She might not have recognized it if Thibodeaux hadn't given her and Meg a ride in it last fall. Sure enough, the profile behind the wheel belonged to the overly serious detective.

Sabine's eyes watered with an unwelcome emotion. She ducked her chin and blinked to clear them. When she looked again, the car was gone. Her chest ached. Maybe she'd been working too hard, pulled a muscle. She blew her nose on a black T-shirt with the words "Grab Your Brooms. We Ride At Dawn" printed in bright white letters on the front.

Throwing it behind the counter, she got back to work. A novelty for her. She normally found it more convenient to borrow what she needed, when she needed it, rather than bother laboring for it beforehand. Much more efficient than all this mucking about with manual labor. If you could call folding T-shirts and gathering bins full of crystal necklaces off the floor as manual labor. And she did.

Why else would her chest ache?

By 10:00 am, opening time for the Sassy Witch on Fridays, Sabine had everything back in its place. Or, back in *a place*, she might have rearranged things a bit. Rather than divide the crystals in their bins by color, she simply hung them around the neck of the naked manikin standing in the window. The T-shirts she draped over the outstretched arms of the same sexless faux personage.

Cartons of tarot had spilled their contents across the floor. Sabine located the empty boxes and stuffed as many cards as she could into each, with no consideration to which deck they'd originally belonged to. She didn't believe in segregation. If mixed cards wanted to inhabit the same box, who was she to judge?

Future patrons ought to thank her.

How could you know if a tarot reading was accurate if every deck had its own set of cards? This way, it was truly random, up to fate. If you're going to argue with fate, you shouldn't be getting a tarot reading, anyway.

The extra cards, she just pocketed. It was not stealing; she argued with the absent Meg. No box to put them in, anyway. It's efficiency. Should she just throw them away?

Anything she couldn't find a shelf for, she put on the 50% off rack. A sassy little discount.

"You are welcome," Sabine told the empty shop.

If Meg didn't like the setup, she shouldn't play footsy with the Fae. If the shop's owner didn't like it, she shouldn't hire English majors to work a job that obviously required strategic skills only a well-educated thief could provide.

Sabine propped the door open to the smattering of pedestrians out for an early stroll.

The warmer air from inside the shop mingled with the cool, damp air off the river, forming a mist. Quite magical, if she did say so herself.

Throughout the morning, the traffic picked up as the first tourists finished their croissant breakfasts at the café across the street. The shop was packed by noon after the rest of the tourists recovered from their hangovers and ventured out into the light to reenact the day before, presumably ending with a fresh hangover tomorrow morning.

Customers gathered at the counter asking questions and demanding to check out, assuming Sabine was there to help them. She tended to some and ignored others. Most merely mauled the goods and left them in even worse disarray. She'd leave that for Meg to sort out tomorrow. She didn't want to rob her of all the consequences of consorting with otherworldly creatures.

How else would her roommate learn?

Sabine's undying generosity amazed even her.

A bird struck the window, startling her. The crow fluttered to a stop on the sill where it stalked back and forth, peering in. It seemed to catch her eye and opened its beak to speak or squawk or something. Instead, it abruptly snapped it shut and ducked behind the window's manikin.

Sabine was trying to make up her mind as to whether she had imagined it, and if it were the crow from the streetcar, when it poked its head back into view, tapped the glass, and ducked back out of sight.

"What the devil?" Sabine asked.

"Tsk-Tsk. 'Tis no *diable*, but Mlle. Georgette."

Sabine swung around to find the eerie woman from the cemetery standing directly behind her. She wore a near identical outfit to the one she had on yesterday. Except this one was dark green rather than burgundy, with a matching brocade, thigh length swing coat. Her nails bronze rather than pewter. The Creole woman looked at home in the Sassy Witch.

How had she snuck up on Sabine so easily?

"Clever *le bébé sorcière*, seeking out Georgette's *tutelle*." The woman's propensity to refer to herself in the third person was annoying. And sprinkling in French as if everyone should speak her language was so . . . American of her.

Sabine had looked up that first part after their last encounter in the cemetery. "I am *not* a baby witch." I'm no witch at all, she thought, but didn't share. She took a wild guess as to the meaning of the rest of the sentence. "And I don't need tulle. I grew out of tutus a long time ago."

The woman pealed with laughter. As in, her laugh actually rang out like the clanging of bells. The whole shop froze, startled by the sound. Except they forgot to unfreeze. The shoppers stood unnaturally still.

"Could you unfreeze them? That's just creepy." *And you are already creepy enough.*

"My *clientèle* does not come to witness your education, *ma petite.*"

"This is *your* shop? You're the Sassy Witch?" Sabine wanted to laugh, but her heart beat against the cage of her ribs like a trapped bird, and her throat threatened to close up. *Why did this woman terrify her? Other than those metallic nails.*

You should need a permit to wear those things.

Georgette rolled her eyes a little too hard. They went full on white for a second before focusing like lasers on Sabine. "You are not as *stupide* as you act."

"I'm not stupid at all. I've just never met another witch, other than—" Sabine cut herself off. Who knew what this woman, this witch, might do with the information that Sabine was related to the Domingue witches? "What makes you think I need teaching?"

"Your overripe energy wafts off like *parfum pas cher.*"

"English," Sabine said, irritable at being called overripe. Later, when she learned she'd also been compared to cheap perfume, she'd really be pissed.

"*Le nigaud.* I will speak small words for the *ninny.*"

Sabine bristled.

"Oh, so sorry. The baby," Georgette paused to flick an invisible piece of lint from her coat before adding, "witch."

"If I need to learn something from a faux French witch, I'll let you know." Sabine shoved a box of T-shirts out of her way and stormed for the door.

The shoppers instantly thawed, and all converged in front of her. Half-a-head shorter than everyone but a pre-teen girl in pigtails and goth makeup, Sabine couldn't get through the human blockade. She shot a glare at the shop owner.

The pompous Mlle. Georgette returned it with a self-satisfied smirk. "Tell Mlle. Megan she will show up to work tomorrow if she wants to keep her job. Unless you want to come back in her place. Perhaps to practice your baby magic steps."

Sabine saw an opening and shoved her way out, bumping into a handsome young Latino man with a tidy goatee. He broke into a grin.

"How pleasant to run into a lovely lady on my first day of work."

Sabine scowled. This did nothing to deter him.

He gave a chivalrous bow. "Oliver, and you are?"

He was hitting on her! She did not have the time or the patience for this.

"I am leaving," she barked and elbowed him aside. He just chuckled and continued in. Idiot.

She was done with this shop and helping Meg. If her roommate couldn't keep herself away from the Fae, maybe she should ask them for a job.

Craaw-Craaw. Black wings assaulted Sabine as she plowed down the street.

"What the—" she halted, beak to nose with a crow clinging to the side of the iron column where the Creole man had stood earlier in the morning. They studied one another. Sabine squinting her eyes. The crow rotating its head to lay one beady eye then the other upon her.

Is it you? She couldn't bring herself to ask out loud.

After a man in a Hawaiian print shirt and flip-flops passed them, the bird ventured a *Creeek*?

"Stupid crow shaped feather duster," Sabine said, but her heart wasn't in it as she waved the bird off the column.

C-r-r-runk. The bird batted her about the head with its wings before soaring away.

Sabine's eyes burned with that same unwelcome emotion. Swiping them with the back of her hand, she stormed home to fuss at Meg. She'd come up with a passable reason by the time she got there.

Chapter 6

THIBODEAUX

Singed muscle and bone encapsulated the cavity just to the left of center in the cadaver's chest. Frigid air from the AC blew directly over the examination table, dampening the smell of char. It raised goosebumps along Detective Thibodeaux's arms beneath his button-up shirt and blazer. He'd requested to be present during the autopsy.

Jean-Luc's stomach soured.

He normally had an ironclad constitution from years of eating his mother's jambalaya—voted spiciest in the parish by anyone who wanted a second helping, as well as those who didn't. And his Uncle Harold's chili—voted 2nd spiciest in the parish Chili Festival of 2017. Later years' winners were deemed irrelevant by all Thibodeaux family members in good standing.

During Jean-Luc's time in the New Orleans Police Department, he'd witnessed fresh gunshot wounds ranging from a Saturday night disagreement concerning the SEC—which occurred too frequently amongst God fearing football fans who ought to know better. To a territorial gang shootout—thank the good Lord and the NOPD Homicide Squad these shootings were down in recent years. He'd pulled bloated bodies from the mighty Mississippi River, from the murky Bayou Saint-Jean, and from bloody bathtubs. And he'd seen bodies burnt in house fires, in car wrecks, and from immolation.

Nope, he didn't have a weak stomach. But something about this cadaver had his lunch considering making a hasty exit.

The medical examiner, speaking in monotone, recited exactly what those reasons might be.

Although a transcript of the report would be sent to his office, Jean-Luc took down as many facts as he could. Not as precise as the examiner, but it was God awful enough in shorthand.

- Strips of skin and muscle, approximately 2 cm by 5 cm, torn from face, chest, arms, and legs.

- Cavity in chest 5 cm left of center, approximately 8 cm by 4 cm. Skin and muscle missing.

- Five puncture wounds, at intervals consistent with that of the spread of human fingers and thumb, mark entry points. Wounds cauterized.

- Torn skin surrounding the cavity, torn and charred.

- Sternum broken, caved into cavity, blackened conducive to high heat of approximately 400 - 550 degrees Celsius.

- Three ribs on the left splintered and charred. White color indicated a heat of approximately 900 - 1000 degrees Celsius.

- Rib fragments missing.

- Heart missing.

- Coronary arteries and veins cauterized.

- Sixth degree burns on adjacent organs, tendons, and bone.

Sweat beaded on Jean-Luc's upper lip and he brushed it away with the cuff of his shirt. Swallowing hard, he kept his eyes pinned on his notebook as the examiner continued to list facts. She had yet to cut the cadaver open when Jean-Luc received a call and excused himself.

Pacing to the end of the corridor, he finished up, headed back for the exam room, and came face to face with his assistant. "Carmichael, what'd you need?"

Shifting her weight and moving her purse from one side to the other, she took a beat before answering. "I got a call about a disturbance at the French Market and thought I'd stop by here on my way back to see how things were going."

"A bit out of the way," he said before thinking better of it. "All's well. She's still working?"

"She?" Carmichael asked.

"The forensics pathologist."

"A woman, huh," she said distractedly. An odd comment for a female officer who'd worked her way up through the ranks and was preparing to take the written and physical agility tests to become a detective within the next couple of months. "He—she give you any idea what happened? Some drug deal gone wrong, and they decide to carve his heart out?"

"What have I told you about jumping to conclusions?"

Her head twitched, and her brow furrowed. "What? Oh, yeah. Wait until you've seen all you can see and heard all you can hear. Right. So, what's up in there?"

Jean-Luc waved for her to follow as he went for coffee at the nurse's station. He poured a cup, handed it to her, and poured another, buying time as he decided what to share. She'd see the report eventually, and he had no solid reason to distrust her motives.

Other than her intervention at the morgue last fall.

He gave her the short version.

"Chest cavity, heart missing."

She nodded along.

"Sternum caved in."

"Caved in, not splayed out?" she asked, confused.

"Yes. Like a mallet or something caved it in."

Her brow pinched again, and she shifted her purse back to the other shoulder, juggling her coffee, and remarkably spilling neither.

Jean-Luc continued watching the minute shifts in her expression. "It was hard to see in the dim light this morning, but the cavity was burned. Everything cauterized. Bone cooked almost to dust."

Carmichael startled at the information and took a step back. Jean-Luc hadn't known her to be skittish before. Her eyes darted back and forth as if searching for something. Noticing him watching, she ducked her head, hiding her expression.

"Sorry if that's too much detail. We can wait for the report for the rest."

"No, no. That's fine. It just sounds so inhuman, right? Someone steals his heart and burns his insides. For what? To hide evidence? It's not like we could've gotten a fingerprint from in there." She paced as she talked.

Jean-Luc caught her by the elbow to slow her down. Her purse slipped, jerking her arm, and the coffee hit the floor. They both knelt at once to clean it up, bumping heads.

"I'm sorry." He grabbed a wad of paper towels from over the sink and passed them to her as she scrubbed at her pants.

"No problem. They're black. Hides all kinds of things." She chuckled, but her face was still pinched. Eyes tight, mouth flatlined.

"I'll let the examiner know we're leaving, and I'll walk you to your car."

"No, no," she repeated. "You stay. I'll see you back at the precinct." Carmichael made her way to the elevator and jabbed at the button. She gave him a strained smile and resumed pacing until the door dinged open.

When Jean-Luc returned, the examiner, an older woman in her fifties, maybe sixties, was cutting a line down from the gaping hole to the cadaver's navel. He swallowed hard and asked, "What do you think could burn a man like that? Burn his heart out and not burn the rest of him to ash?"

She placed the scalpel on the tray before answering. "I have not concluded that the heart was burnt out. No residue is remaining. It might have been removed, and the arteries cauterized simultaneously, which would explain the amount of blood remaining in the body."

The bile rose in his throat, and he swallowed again. "All right. Let's say the heart was taken. The bones are broken inward. What could do that? A sledgehammer, maybe?"

"Possibly one was used to break the bone, but the torn skin is not conducive to a hammer strike." She turned back to her work, peeling the skin away and removing each organ, one at a time. Weighing each, recording the results and placing them on a second table.

Jean-Luc's voice was husky as he spoke. "And the burning at such high temperatures? What could cause that?"

Her hands stilled, and she peered at him over her spectacles. "A white-hot rage."

He laughed.

She did not.

Chapter 7

WARWICK

As the quarter moon rose, the Faerie Market woke from a week-long slumber. Faeflies pulsed in a syncopated rhythm like the flip side of jazz. Wings buzzed in harmony. Marble statues turned to watch the odd creatures venturing between booths. A female with warm sienna skin and antelope horns carried a basket filled with carved masks. A male, tall and willowy, glided by carrying brightly colored silks which fluttered past his wings.

The waking market was a wonder to behold, even to the goblin Warwick. Even after all these years.

Colors unseen in the human world flowed on currents from hidden crystals. Energy vibrated through the air. Silver, gold, and enameled armor flexed for the admiration of the first shoppers to arrive. Short swords cut through crystal fruits, exposing both for examination.

Warwick would have stopped to witness the blooming market if he didn't have to ready his own booth for customers.

Warwick placed his more valuable, easily stolen items on the table facing the center of the market. The slippery, enchanted chains slithered through his gnarled fingers as he arranged them on velvet pads. His eye crinkled around his jeweler's loupe as he examined a miniature vial dangling from a chain. Deep within, purple light swirled in a frantic spiral as if looking for a way out. Hanging it on the wire tree created to keep such baubles contained, he went to the far side of his booth to retrieve the rarer pieces of his collection.

The dark heart of the market cast a shadow over the jewels in their new position. They didn't glitter quite as bright here, but he chose to face the pulsing darkness rather than turn his back on it, lest it come for him.

Each quarter, his booth slid closer to the center of the Faerie Market. It pulled him in as if it hungered for him. Every vendor felt the pull, the slow slide into peril. They couldn't all fit in the center, he reasoned with himself. Not unless some disappeared, lost to the void.

Warwick did not plan on being one of them. He was a clever goblin. He'd taken to wearing his jeweler's loupe positioned over his eye at all times. Even with its enchantments, he could not see what dwelled in the depths of that darkness, but he'd see what came out of it.

The darkness heaved a great exhale, and a figure stepped out into the market. Their eyes shifted as if sizing up their next victim. They wore a red cap which glistened as if freshly dipped in blood. Rivulets dripped down the forest green cloak and splattered crimson droplets on the ground, leaving a trail as the creature passed.

Warwick averted his eyes. No one wanted to trigger a Redcap unnecessarily. And he could think of no necessity.

With his head ducked, he felt rather than saw a familiar patron at his booth. Ice crystals formed in the air and fell like snow to adorn the necklaces laid out on velvet cushions. Warwick knew better than to lift his eyes to the cloaked figure.

"I see you seek favor with the heart of the market," the creature said with an ugly chuckle.

Warwick swallowed a lump lodged in his throat and chose to remain quiet rather than correct the ill wind that had blown his way. They knew he had not chosen this position. Instead, he asked, "May I be of service?"

"I have need of another timepiece. Same spells. Same arrangement."

The voice alone was enough to chill the blood in Warwick's veins. His extremities went cold as ice, and his heart beat twice as hard. The joints of his gnarled fingers ached as he plucked a thick brass chain from a stand and held it out. A spherical timepiece dangled from it, catching the light.

A gloved hand cupped the bauble and ran a thumb over its curve. The clock inside spun forward faster and faster. The hands counted out seconds, minutes, hours until they were a blur. Warwick felt the days and nights wound tight into the spring within.

Pity swelled in his calcified heart, a feeling he had not held in an age. Whatever poor fool received this gift would be trapped in a torturous state until the time spun out. If they survived that long.

Jewels from the Goblin Court were drawn from the creature's robes as payment. Warwick snatched them up greedily, ignoring any pangs of guilt arising from his part in the transaction. He was only a vendor, after all.

What the creature chose to do with his wares once they exchanged hands was not Warwick's business. It was not as if he had a choice. Not anymore. Not after the first deal was struck. He'd been paid for his silence and his continued service. The choice on that first night, moons ago, also bound him tonight and to all future nights, unending, unless someone put a stop to the insanity. But it would not be him.

The air warmed as the creature moved away. Warwick dared a glance up. The hood revealed nothing but darkness. The creature's face was hidden by powerful spells just as before. But Warwick knew to whom he sold the enchanted piece.

May the darkness preserve him. He knew.

Busying himself by resorting the merchandise, Warwick was startled when a crow with iridescent wings landed atop the wire tree. It twisted its shiny head, focused a beady eye on Warwick, then began picking through the jewelry hanging from the branches. It picked off a spiral of sea glass beads and dropped it. Its sharp beak sorted through the collection and plucked a circular earring hung with freshwater pearls. Slate blue, a silvery Bordeaux, and an inky violet. The colors matched the bird's feathers.

Creeeck? it asked.

Stealing in the Faerie Market could get you thrown out, slaughtered, or worse. Gifted items bound the giver and receiver until the deal was broken. Warwick had more entanglements than he could currently handle.

Reluctantly, he started to shake his head when the crow ruffled its feathers and dropped a crescent moon charm. It clinked into a crystal goblet holding loose beads. The crow bobbed its head.

Warwick's eyes darted around to see if there were any witnesses to the interaction. He whispered a word of concealment, slid the moon charm into his pocket, and gave the crow a curt nod.

"Fair be thy luck, my dark friend."

Tok-tok-tok. The crow ticked at him, ducked its head into the loop of the hoop earring, and fluffed its feathers. The silver wire settled beneath its ruff while the pearls blended into the feathers on its chest. It launched, soaring through the branching arms supporting the roof of the market, silently disappearing into the night beyond.

Warwick took a deep breath, hoping he'd cured more trouble than he'd caused.

A bone-jarring reverberation shook the table before him. Chains slithered off their perches. Crystal shattered against the floor. The gloom across the aisle broke open.

Light cracked the darkness, exposing the human market beyond. The brilliant daylight of their reality dazzled his vision before the gloom fell upon it, consuming the light and everything within. Warwick's tables and racks collapsed. The display tables were dragged toward the gaping maw, but the darkness's hunger was not sated.

Warwicking scrabbled for purchase as he plummeted into the black heart of the Faerie Market.

Chapter 8

MEGAN

The sky faded to black, and the streetlights startled awake. Meg had just finished up a grueling week at the Sassy Witch where the owner, in her hot goth girl outfit, stood guard as Meg cleaned up the mess Sabine had made. It took days to put everything back in order. Just sorting the tarot cards alone had taken two, and she wasn't brave enough to tell Georgette, the owner, that some cards were still missing.

Meg locked up the door to the shop. Georgette had already 'retired' upstairs to her 'boudoir.' Meg could hardly understand her half the time, but she understood that at least. The new guy, Oliver, slouched against a metal column watching.

"Did you leave something inside?" she asked. His lazy smile said that wasn't the problem.

"I'm headed over to the warehouse to help finish up work on our float for the parade. Want to tag along?"

"I'm good." She actually wanted to go home and vent to Sabine about what a *witch* Georgette was about the whole mess.

"Come. It'll be fun. We'll pick up a couple of six packs on the way. You know you need to wind down after a day with her." His eyes rotated up to the apartment above the shop.

Was he flirting with her? Surely not.

Meg shook her head.

Undaunted, Oliver waggled his eyebrows. "The float this year is Eros, the Roman god of love and desire."

The Greek god of love, desire, and fertility, Meg mentally corrected him, but decided it was best to keep the correction to herself. "Thanks, but my roommate's holding supper for me."

Which was a blatant lie. Sabine never waited on anyone to eat. Plus, she probably wouldn't even be home until the crowds on Bourbon thinned out. Which they never seemed to this time of year. Still, she was tired and wanted to go home. And was definitely not interested in flirting.

"All right," he said good-naturedly. He headed off with a wave over his shoulder. "I'll catch you at work tomorrow."

Meg nodded and crossed the street, headed home. A click from above caught her attention. Georgette stood on the balcony, watching. She leaned on the railing with her head in one hand, while the other hand clicked long metallic nails against the cast iron.

Meg waved goodbye and turned to make her way down the sidewalk. A sharp snap hit the center of her spine and ran through it like electricity. It felt like one of Sabine's practice shots. Unnerved, Meg refused to look back. Although the feeling evaporated once she'd turned the corner, Meg wriggled her shoulders and picked up her pace.

Parking near the shop was a pain at any time of year, but this close to Mardi Gras, it was impossible. The walk home wasn't too bad, and panhandlers mostly left her alone. Maybe it was her height. Maybe they saw her leaving the Sassy Witch shop and assumed her income didn't allow for handouts.

An inhumanly tall and lovely man fell into step with her. A chilled wind blew strands of hair across her cheek. She picked up her pace, and so did he, matching her stride with ease. He wasn't taking the hint.

So she came to an abrupt halt and asked, "Excuse me, have we met before?"

"My little pet, you do not remember me?" His smile was predatory and sexy at once. A very dangerous combination.

"Should I?" she asked, her voice breathier than she'd have liked.

The ice in his crystal blue eyes should have frozen the blood solid in her veins. Instead, it sent a flush up her neck and over her cheeks as if her skin remembered their touch. Maybe it did, but she didn't. Her memories of the Fae disappeared with the charm bracelet.

Meg remembered remembering. Images flitted in her mind's eye like captive fireflies going dark. She recalled returning home each time a bit dopey, but seemingly no worse for the wear. No discernible negative consequences if you don't count compromising her job, therefore her paycheck, ergo her rent. But really not much beyond that.

"And your name is?" Meg asked.

"You may call me Baylur."

"Oh, may I?" Meg tried for some of Sabine's snark, but didn't pull it off with the quiver in her voice. "And we've met where?"

"For the first time in the Midnight Jazz Club." His feral grin grew wider, showing teeth that were a little too sharp. Meg reached for her ear as if she had felt the scrape of them against her lobe before. "Last time was in the halls of the ice giants where I peeled your clothes—"

"Yeah, yeah. That checks out." Meg stopped him.

Her skin had pebbled with goosebumps from the nape of her neck and torso to, well, to too low. She could feel his words were true, even with the gaps in her memory, the images lost without the charms. The club she remembered because she'd gone back with Sabine to look for Valdi. That time, she hadn't been intoxicated by the Fae's influence.

Sabine had been right, though. Last week wasn't Meg's first or even second trip to the In Between since she discovered it last fall. She remembered the aftereffects, if not the actual hookups.

After the Fae took Valdi from her, Meg had sworn never to go back to the Midnight Jazz Club or the Faerie Market. Her best friend had gone voluntarily, sure, but she was still gone, leaving Meg with the snarky little witch, Sabine, who barely had enough magic to fill a shot glass.

After losing Valdi to the mysteries of the hidden creatures of New Orleans, Meg swore off the arcane, the mysterious, and the supernatural. But living in the Big Easy made it hard to keep that oath.

She stifled a laugh at the irony. A cool hand wrapped around her waist and tightened, chilling the laugh in her chest.

"So, back to the club?" Meg eked out.

"The Midnight is too tame for us, my pet. The In Between has many doors. We shall choose another." He shifted out of the lamplight, becoming hardly more than a silhouette. The tall Fae's shadowed features turned ominous. His sharp smile glinted from the remnants of light from the moon.

Another shiver ran down her spine. Meg remained in the cone of light, resisting the tug of his hand. "I should go home first and leave Sabine a note."

"The tiny thief? She does not think of you. Not as I do."

"She'll worry," Meg protested.

Maybe she would, maybe she wouldn't. Sabine sure griped enough about Meg being out all night. Meg hadn't asked for her to fill in at the shop. That had been her choice. And Meg had paid the price for it.

Baylur cocked an eyebrow. "My sweet, you measure her against yourself. And she does not measure up. The witchling cares for herself and no one else. Does she not come and go as she pleases?"

Had Meg told him about Sabine before? Was he stalking her, or her roommate?

The more Meg thought it through, the more right it felt. She envied Sabine's bravado. The foxy little woman came and went as she pleased, just like he said. Sabine, adrift on her own wind, created hurricanes in her wake. Leaving everyone else to swirl in the eddies left behind, trying not to drown.

Delicately, Baylur lifted Meg's chin with a fingertip, putting their lips barely a breath apart. "My petite, I watch out for you. I and no one else."

That jolted her. It was almost certainly not true, but all the faces that popped into her mind lent credence to what he said. Valdi, her former roommate and best friend, had left. Sabine came and went. Meg's parents and their horde of children had all dispersed over the years, leaving Meg to basically raise herself. And no boyfriend had ever stuck around for long.

But this Fae, he came back for her.

"You said I fascinate you," she remembered.

"Indeed, you do. Come away with me. I shall be your sole focus and you shall be mine." His cool breath brushed her lips, and she leaned in.

The razor edge of his teeth caught her bottom lip. Meg tasted her own blood, warm and salty on her tongue, mingled with the moss and moonlight taste of him. Her breath caught, and she thought she might lose it entirely when he pulled away and took her arm.

"I have wonders to share with you. And you shall be mine?" Baylur repeated, and she forgot to be afraid of what that might mean.

She might not remember where they had been together, but he was so lovely to look at and he called her *little* and *petite* and *mine*. She didn't remember any pair of eyes studying her before, as his did. Despite her height, she was rarely noticed at all.

Valdi had noticed her, she reminded herself.

But Valdi was gone.

Sabine had moved in, but only because she needed a place to stay. Sure, she'd inherited her aunt's house, but Sabine couldn't bring herself to clean the blood off her aunt's kitchen floor. No, the little thief did not give a shit about Meg.

This man made her skin tingle at a mere glance. Her body remembered his touch. He came for her, even though she couldn't remember his name. He sought her out, again and again.

"I shall be yours." If only for tonight. She hugged his arm tight to her chest.

His tender smile grew large and perhaps the tiniest bit wolfish. Wider still, and it was most definitely wolfish.

Hot.

Scary, but still HOT.

Meg fairly floated, an experience foreign to her, since she normally lumbered among people all shorter than her.

Baylur led her down narrow streets she didn't remember existing in the historic Vieux Carre district, but she'd only lived there for a few months. Surely there were many parts left for her to explore. They turned down a dead end, which she hadn't known to exist in this gridded area of town. But who was she to question her guide?

At the end, a door opened, framing a crooked man, arms and legs all akimbo. He wore a leer.

Fear spiked, and she drew back. The man chuckled, low and nasty. Baylur echoed the sound. Putting a firm hand to her back, he maneuvered her past the crooked man. Her arm brushed against him, and she recoiled. Baylur stood at her back, preventing her escape.

The door shut behind her, and the corridor ahead grew long and dark. Its far end lost to the darkness. The void boiled with eyes and teeth, tails and talons.

The breath caught in Meg's throat. This time, it was not Baylur's lovely face that had stolen her breath. His expression had become feral and hungry. His predatory eyes fixed on her.

Meg remembered that look. And screamed.

Chapter 9

SABINE

Sabine came home to an empty apartment. No surprise. Meg must've gone gallivanting with the Fae again. They had their claws in her. But Meg always slipped free. Sabine had never heard of anyone so enamored with the Fae who could also slip from their grasp so easily come morning.

So, Sabine emptied her evening's loot from the leather satchel she carried on her expeditions and into the trunk she'd inherited from Meg's previous roommate, Valdi. Thoughtful of the woman to leave it and all her other belongings, as meager as they might be, for Sabine's use. She inventoried her haul, almost enough to make her half of the rent, and went to bed, worrying needlessly for her roommate's wellbeing.

Morning came. Sabine made a full pot of coffee and warmed an extra day-old pastry. One for her, one for a hung-over Meg who was due through the door any minute. Then Sabine sat on the back of the couch, waiting for the clattering sound of Meg searching through her purse for her keys. Sabine had the timing down pat. She could open the door just as Meg's keys reached the lock. Sabine deserved her small amusements.

Except the morning came and went without Meg stumbling up the stairs.

Sabine took a break from her vigil to eat the second scone, ignoring the crow battering against the window. The oversized clock on the wall whirled past another hour. Sabine gave up and took a shower. Meg could just sit on the landing until she got out, or figure out how to use a lock and key for herself.

Sabine took her time. When she finished securing her auburn ponytail at the back of her head, the clock ticked past opening time for the Sassy Witch. Meg must've gone straight to work in day-old clothes and Fae-mussed hair. That would tick off the fussy French witch that ran the shop, which suited Sabine just fine.

Maybe she ought to stop by to harass her roommate for worrying her. Not that she was actually worried. But needling her in front of her boss would be satisfying. Not that she wanted to face the corseted witch. How stereotypical could you get? Sabine went for the last scone before leaving, but realized she'd already eaten it.

Well, nothing for it but to get her day started. The tourists of the French Quarter weren't going to fleece themselves. Well, they might. But those spoils were rightfully hers. She owned that turf, not any newcomer wanna-be thief.

The crow was nowhere to be found when she exited the cottage that housed their apartment. Not that she cared. The pedestrian traffic was slim pickings on the way toward the river, middle of the week and all. Plus, Sabine was distracted. Maybe she was the tiniest bit worried. She'd make Meg pay for that once she got to the shop.

Sabine sauntered through the open door. The handsome, Latino man she'd run into before stood behind the counter ringing up customers. Oliver gave her his best salesmen-schmoozy smile.

"Welcome to the Sassy Witch," he greeted her, obviously not remembering their run-in.

Mlle. Georgette stood in the opening to the back stairs, glaring.

"You can tell the tall one that her service *est fini*," the witch said. Georgette moved the young man to the side and efficiently rang up a shopper without looking at the person or what they bought. Oliver stepped aside, still wearing the slick smile, oblivious to his boss's current disposition.

Today, the wicked witch wore her usual uniform, but in a deep plum and no brocade coat. For adornment, her nails were lacquered gold, and she wore a gold dangly bracelet. As on that day in the cemetery, her chest looked damp. Maybe a brunch accident, and not trusting the pretty boy to run the shop for her, she couldn't change.

Sabine would take care of that and save Meg's ass in the process.

"Ms. Armand sent me in her place this morning."

The witch slitted her eyes at Sabine while handing the customer a gift bag and waving her away. "So, you have come for your lessons. *Choix intelligente*, but *stupide* to arrive late when begging for my help."

Beg? Play it cool, Sabine. You are here to save Meg's job.

Georgette gestured for Sabine to get behind the counter and tend to the next customer. She did, but slow enough to irritate both the shopper and her pseudo-employer. Sabine gave Georgette a winning smile and a less gracious one to Oliver who'd wheedled his way into Meg's job.

Georgette hooked a finger in his collar and left back through the back door with him in tow.

"Hey, what about those lessons you planned to force on me?" Sabine called after her with no answer. Georgette did not reappear, nor did her new boy toy. With that pretty face, one could only assume, and Sabine did.

A foot shorter than the customer across the counter, Sabine glowered up at him, letting him know he was to blame for the delay, not her. The man sneered, but backed down when Sabine put a little hex in her eyes. A little was all she had. His brow broke out in a sweat as he grabbed his bag and quickly left.

The rest of the day went pretty much the same, with Sabine barking at any shopper who lingered too long at the counter, wanting to chat about the authenticity of the shop and its owner. She expected Georgette and the boy toy, Oliver, back after lunch; they weren't. She expected Meg in, begging forgiveness any minute. She didn't. Leaving Sabine to ring up and bag merchandise.

If she couldn't see the pricing signs from behind the counter, she just put in a miscellaneous number. Sometimes, she guessed low, served the fussy witch right. Sometimes, she knowingly went high and pocketed the difference. Compensation for her trouble. Hazard pay, if you will. Even if you won't, because there was no one in the shop to stop her.

By late afternoon, Sabine had grown bored and waved a couple out the door without charging them. Sparks flared around the opening, shoving them back inside. Blue lightning arced off the door until the two dropped their armload of goods. They sat stunned for a moment before jumping to their feet and fleeing, T-shirts and magnets forgotten.

The next customer that Sabine bothered to ring up left her card in the card reader as it dinged at her. Leaving her scented oils and faux Voodoo doll keyring, too, the woman went to the door to see why a string of people ran by the shop. Probably worried she was missing out on one of the parades leading up to the big Mardi Gras blowout.

Sabine, considerate as ever, pocketed the card and shoved the merchandise under the counter. Leave a fox alone in the henhouse, you come up a few eggs short.

Sirens blared, heading towards the shop.

Maybe the police didn't agree with Sabine's assessment about eggs and henhouses. But they barreled through the intersection without slowing.

Their blue lights flickered between the patrons, but Sabine couldn't see over the customers' heads to spot which way the police were headed. It sounded like they were going towards the market. At mid-afternoon, what trouble could there be other than an amateur pickpocket or two?

A ripple of information cascaded through the shop. Before it reached Sabine, the shoppers turned en masse and exited. They joined the throngs on the sidewalk, pointing into the sky.

Sabine followed, but couldn't get through the wall of people. Nor could she see over them. She climbed into the window box beside the manikin and steadied herself with a hand on the figure's shoulder. On tiptoes, she peered through the crack between the balcony above and the heads below.

Shoppers clogged the doorway and speculated on the cause.

"The French Market?"

"It's on fire!"

"All that black smoke must be a car."

That was no car fire.

A column of black smoke billowed up, marring the bright blue sky. Monstrous forms roiled within the dark plume, threatening to burst forth, but the cloud consumed them before they could break free.

It was certainly supernatural and, therefore, did not belong on this side of the Beyond.

She'd better go see about it, Sabine told herself. With a well-rehearsed sigh of altruism, she squirmed through the matted knot of pedestrians and headed straight for trouble. It was, after all, one of her specialties.

Around the corner, the French Market came into view.

People screaming.

Firetrucks blaring.

Smoke billowing into the air.

Raiders making away with stolen goods amidst the chaos.

And one very gnarled goblin shot forth onto the sidewalk as if expelled from the belly of a great beast. He landed on his derrière, bounced once, got his stubby legs under him, and ran headlong into her. They tussled about a bit before they could untangle their limbs and sort themselves out.

The round-eyed goblin made to run, but stopped to gawk at Sabine, who gawked back at him.

"Are you?" Sabine asked, meaning, *Are you Warwick, the goblin vendor who gave Meg, who's now missing, a charm bracelet that has simultaneously caused and cured one trauma after another?*

He responded, "You!" Meaning, *You!*

Or so Sabine assumed.

"You conniving little sneak thief," he clarified.

So she'd guessed right.

"Warwick? What are you doing on this side of the In Between?"

"Hopefully hiding," he said, searching wildly about for a goblin sized hiding spot.

While he tried to squeeze between a chalkboard describing the outer wall of the bar on the corner and the wicked hoppiness of the beers on tap, Thibodeaux's car pulled up alongside the curb. The detective got out and observed the officers trying to herd panicky people. Sabine stepped between him and the goblin just before he noticed her.

A confusion of emotions played across his face before he settled on his professional mask. "Sabine, did you see what happened?" By which he meant, *Did you* cause *what happened?*

Sabine folded her arms and spoke over the grumbles of the poorly hidden goblin behind her. "See what?"

His face hardened as Detective Thibodeaux pointed at the billowing cloud behind him. The writhing mass of creatures roiling within it collapsed into the black smoke as it receded towards the center of the market. Within a heartbeat, the sky had cleared.

Sabine shrugged.

The detective's expression grew as dark as the disappearing cloud. He whipped around, ready to march into the fray when he looked up to witness the bright blue sky. Shoppers froze, stunned. Looters paused long enough for police officers to snap back to attention and close in. The would-be criminals dropped their armloads of stolen goods and ran.

Taking advantage of the moment's distraction, Sabine hauled the goblin out of his hiding place and shoved him inside a mask shop where he could pose as a manikin if necessary.

Chapter 10

THIBODEAUX

Black vapors sank from the tar-like substance, coating the underside of the French Market's canopy. The air had a gritty, burnt-tire taste that clung to Jean-Luc's tongue despite the bottle of water he'd bought from an overpriced vendor. Officers circled the burnt booths underneath. More than one held a handkerchief to their mouth and nose. The woman beside him blinked rapidly, her eyes watering from the noxious air.

At least he wasn't the only one seeing black mists this time. A small measure of relief in an otherwise cursed day. And surprise, surprise, Sabine's there to observe it. Again.

How many crimes could she "witness" before he had to consider her a prime suspect, or at least an instigator? But how could Sabine, witch or no, have caused something like this? How could anyone? In the middle of the market? In the middle of the day?

But somehow, all magical lunacy tied back to her.

Bad luck? Absolutely. But his? Or hers?

A total of six people were reported missing so far, presumedly consumed in the explosion. An Asian couple in their mid-50s, early 60s, had disappeared into the plume of black smoke. A pushy man in his mid-40s was also reported missing. A Middle Eastern woman wept in the arms of another vendor. A young woman who spoke broken English tried to translate the hysterical woman's sobs to the detective.

"It's her son. It gobbled him up."

"The cloud?" Jean-Luc asked.

"She says it was the monsters. The monsters grabbed him and ate him. They pulled him into the smoke, and they ate him," the woman told him. Her eyes were wide, and her face tear-tracked. She, too, began to sob.

"I'm gonna need you to describe these monsters, ma'am."

The mother shook and screamed in anguish.

Jean-Luc made himself take a beat before speaking again. "Going to give you a minute. I know you're upset. But if we're going to get your son back, I'm going to need some more details, okay?"

The woman nodded, then hid her face in the other woman's shoulder. The other vendor stroked her long ponytail and murmured words of solace to her, while looking wide-eyed over her head at the detective.

"Thibodeaux. Detective Thibodeaux," one of his officers called to him from the edge of the taped off area.

He mouthed, "I'll be back," to the woman, and she closed her eyes, leaning her temple against the grieving mother's head.

A sanitation worker wove between the circle of sidewalk gawkers and officers and passed a blunt-nosed shovel over the police tape to Jean-Luc. He nodded his thanks, handed his water bottle to a nearby officer, and positioned the blade at the edge of the black sludge marking the blast zone. Setting his feet, he rammed the shovel under the simmering tar.

It wedged under an inch and stopped. The shovel's nose began to sizzle. Corrosion crawled up the metal. It crusted over with rust as they watched. The end cracked and broke loose. The piece in contact with the tar-like substance disintegrated into a fine red powder.

Gasps, hisses, moans, and screams erupted from the onlookers. Some shoved forward, held back by the police. Others rushed back, stumbling over each other in their haste to get away. Amongst all the varied exclamations, the janitor next to the detective spoke up. "How am I supposed to clean that up? I can't is how. They can't expect me to clean that."

An officer told him, "Nobody expects you to."

Jean-Luc didn't know if that was true. Who knew what the owners of the French market expected? Whether they wanted it or not. It didn't look like it could be cleaned up anytime soon. But he could take this one worry off the janitor's shoulders for now.

"This is an active crime scene. No one is to come close to this residue until we determine where it came from and how it can be safely removed."

The janitor's shoulders relaxed, and he backed away, merging with the crowd.

The tar continued to bulge and grow like a slow-moving lava flow while the center steamed with black smoke, evaporating from the middle out. The vendors around the perimeter of the incident pulled away tables and packed up goods in a rush, not knowing whether the ooze would reach them before evaporating.

Hell. Would it eat up the rest of the market and spill out into the streets to eat up up cars and shops before dissipating.

Ducking under the police tape, he went to a vendor who'd been corralled for questioning. Taking his pad out of his pocket, he flipped to a fresh page, past notes about the body on the Canal streetcar and the mother's description of monsters eating her son.

"Your booth was set up next to this . . ." Jean-Luc didn't know what to call it. "Next to the plume of smoke?"

The tanned man answered with what Jean-Luc thought to be a Greek accent. "Yeah. I was right here. My back was to it. Made a sort of whooshing sound like a gust of air. That's what caught my attention. There was like a . . . like a solid column of smoke going up in the middle of the market."

"Did you see anything inside this column of smoke?"

The man's dark eyes darted back and forth. "It was spiraling. You know, like a tire fire. Swirled up and catching under the roof before it burst through."

"So you didn't see any figures, people, animals, and the smoke?" Jean-Luc was loath to use the word monster. Not so long ago, he wouldn't have believed such a thing existed. But his opinion on that was changing fast.

The vendor ducked his chin and tugged at his shirt. "See something like that? No."

Checking with the remaining vendors who'd flanked the broiling tar pit in the middle received wary responses.

"Roiling black cloud."

"Writing mists."

"Sudden."

"Explosive."

"There and gone."

"From Hell."

"Full of demons."

"There was too much smoke to tell for sure," a shopkeeper said. "Might have been something in there. I couldn't say for sure." She checked with her assistant, whose eyes widened before he looked away. "That's all I can say. The smoke burned. My eyes were watering."

She would no longer meet Jean-Luc's eyes.

A look around showed the other witnesses standing apart from one another instead of discussing what it was they'd seen. After an hour and a half, he had no more useful information than he'd started with.

"So, what do you think happened?" Carmichael asked. She'd been the last on the scene this time, after a call for all available officers. Apparently, she was just not available.

Unlike Sabine.

Snapping his notebook shut, he said, "Sudden billowing smoke shot from the central vendors, consuming, or so the witnesses believe, a group of four booths, six vendors, and no count on how many buyers or passersby were swept up in the volatile eruption. Explosion from a leaking gas line is the current theory."

"Whose theory is that?" she asked, lifting a foot to nudge the ooze with the toe of her shoe.

Jean-Luc jerked her back from the tar, but not before the tip of the rubber sole started to bubble and melt. He held her arm as she hopped on one foot and snatched the decomposing shoe off. Her sock had a small hole.

"Let's get you a seat and see about that." Jean-Luc helped her hop over to, and under, the police tape, and to a folding chair

.

at a nearby table. She tore off the sock. Her first two toes were already blistered.

He took a water bottle from a gawker and dumped it over her foot, not knowing if it would do any good. The water sent up a wisp of steam. The rest ran over her foot and down her pant leg. The damage seemed to have stopped, but Carmichael was shaken. Despite the cool weather, sweat dripped from her hairline and ran down her temple.

Jean-Luc handed her a handkerchief. She gave him a shaky smile and blotted her face, then used it to dry off her foot and pants. She handed it back, but he waved it off.

"Keep it."

"What the Hell is that stuff?"

"Hell if I know."

The sludge had stopped its progression, solidifying like a cooling lava flow. A sunbeam cut through the hole in the roof and into the rising black steam. The center of the tar thinned, revealing what looked like a hole cut through the concrete below. Rebar drooped from the melted floor slab.

Maybe it had come from Hell or, "Could it be a rift where lava shot through?"

He was just thinking out loud. As a detective, he knew better than to speculate out loud. The idea caught and spread like a brushfire through the officers, sparks jumping to the witnesses, and flew through the crowd.

"That's it. It must be." Carmichael latched onto the idea, too.

"Have you ever heard of lava spewing from the earth anywhere on the Gulf Coast?" Jean-Luc asked. "Or in the Southeast?"

•

"It's God's vengeance!" came a shout from the far edge, followed by grumbles and groans and some "Amens."

The group shifted and someone stumbled into a middle-aged man who'd been leaning over the police line to get a closeup shot on his phone of the black sludge. He toppled forward, dropping his phone. He dove, grabbing for it as it hit the tar, and started screaming.

The sludge sucked his hand and phone in up to the wrist before Jean-Luc could shove everyone back out of his way. He looped his hands under the man's arm, locked them around his chest, and pulled. The unholy substance pulled back. The man's screams turning into a piercing shriek.

"Help me," Jean-Luc called.

A large, barrel-chested officer stepped in to pull with the detective until the tar ate through to the bone and the man's arm broke free at the elbow. The three men fell back in a heap while the sludge consumed the remnants of the limb, and the injured man went into shock.

The crowd panicked, stampeding out from under the market's canopy. More fell, luckily, away from the tar. Screams ran through like a wave.

"That's it," Jean-Luc roared. "Clear them out. Cordon the entire market until further notice." He snatched a silk scarf from one of the remaining booths nearby and improvised a tourniquet. While EMTs fought their way in through the chaos, and his officers stood by numb with shock.

"Now," he bellowed, "before this turns into a riot."

That snapped them into action.

The NOPD had prepped for the Mardi Gras parades a week in advance. They knew how to cordon off an area and prevent riots.

Even if they couldn't comprehend the black ooze seeping from the earth and consuming people. Or a reported cloud of monsters. Crowd control, they understood.

Chapter 11

MEGAN

The sky beyond the windows was an inky black, a living darkness that writhed and bumped against the glass. Inside, globes bobbed overhead, exuding rays of light that broke against the crystal walls and shattered into colors Meg had never seen before.

As far as she knew, they didn't exist in the world she came from.

But she was not there. She was here. Again.

Her jaw ached from chattering teeth. Her lungs burned from the frigid air. The muscles of her arms were stiff from the cold despite the wrappings. Strips of white linen wrapped tight around her forearms. Damp red lines seeped through, marking the scores in the skin beneath.

Lovely yet terrifying creatures lay about her on divans or sprawled across cushions strewn about the floor. Meg stumbled over and around them as she made her way to the ornate brass doors, nearly twice her height.

How had she gotten here? Her memory slipped and slid so that she had trouble grasping it.

Faces turned to her with vapid smiles. Others had glazed eyes that silently pleaded with her. One creature stood against the wall with a haunted gaze. She could not help them. She had to go. She had somewhere to be. Someone to find.

But who?

A furry paw reached for her, gliding down her calf. Meg stepped free, extended claws snagging at her skin. They cut searing lines across her ankle. But Meg had to go. Someone to find.

A whip-like appendage swept out and encircled her waist. Suckers gripped tight to her exposed midriff. The end plucked at the hem of her shirt. She pulled it free, unwrapping it from her torso.

Someone. But who?

Reaching the exit, she tugged at the door pulls. The cold metal seared her palm and froze to her fingers as she pulled them free. Tearing her fingers free left a layer of skin behind.

Holding the wounded fingers against her chest, Meg searched about for something to use to protect her from the frigid metal. A couple curled around one another beside the door. Their wraps tossed aside, a hinderance in their effort to maximize skin contact with one another.

Well, she needed them. She had to go. And they weren't using them.

Meg scooped them up, their fabric rough against her abraded fingertips. An end knotted in their ankles. She yanked hard, pulling one of their legs aside. One moaned and rolled over, and slung their leg back over their companion.

Wrapping her hands in the ends of the cloth, she grasped the pulls, set her feet, and tugged. The metal door squealed one edge against the other, until it let loose, and the doors sighed open.

She bungled over the couple as she backed up, drawing the door with her.

When it was open enough to allow her to ease through, Meg snapped the wrap out and laid it atop the couple who wriggled together underneath it. Satisfied that she'd done some small good, and grateful for their unknowing contribution, Meg slipped through the doors into a thick blackness.

It enveloped her, choking the air from her.

But she could make it through. She had to.

Meg pushed forward, and a pale figure stepped from the gloom.

Hair of moonlight haloed a cold but beautiful face. The smile, wide and sharp, chilled her to the bone.

She froze in place.

Meg remembered this face.

"My pet," Baylur greeted her. "Looking for me?"

Chapter 12

WARWICK

Naked oak branches provided poor cover, but Warwick was nearly as gnarled as the rough limbs bent from centuries of weathering trauma of one kind or another. His skin gray and mottled and rough. His joints crooked. His nose a knotted snarl. The tree felt more a friend than he thought to find on this side of the In Between. The two of them companions in this strange world of humans.

The battered tree, young by the standards of the Beyond, was ancient on this side. Like Warwick himself. But the tree's great boughs had spent all their time here, its roots in the Beyond. Warwick had grown entirely, limbs and roots, all in the Beyond. The closest he'd hoped to see of this human habitation was the In Between, where he sold his wares at the Faerie Market. A stray human occasionally had the misfortune of stumbling in, but thankfully, it was a rare occurrence.

Breathing in the strange air, Warwick choked back a cough. It tasted flat, no charge, no burble of life.

His ruminations were interrupted by a redheaded woodpecker with a brilliant crest, reminding him of the Redcap in the market. It hammered at a hollow branch riddled with pests, waiting for a strong wind to break free.

"Does it help you to bear it, slamming your head against this dead piece of wood? Should I try it?"

The woodpecker cocked its head to get a closer look at the gnarled piece of wood that spoke. Finding it to be a creature rather than a part of the tree, the bird bid 'adieu' and sprang into the air. The oak gave a sigh of relief and relaxed its hold on the dead branch, which then crashed to the pavers below.

"Whoa! That nearly caved my skull in. Did you do that, Warwick? Are you still up there?"

The shrill voice twanged his elegant, elephantine ears. He considered leaning into the trunk and ignoring the bellowing witch below. She might be an untalented sorceress, but she was proving to be a most persistent pain in his—

"Warwick!"

"What?" he barked back. "You yap like a hound, even in your human form. No wonder the tall one relegated you to the yard."

"Don't be an ass," the mini-witch Sabine called up.

"Don't steal my words," Warwick muttered. He considered waiting for her to demand he come down before moving. After realizing this would make it seem as if he did her bidding, he decided to make a preemptive move and began his descent.

"Get down here," she commanded, right as his booted foot hit the bottom branch. The indignity of having this creature caterwauling at him was enough to decide the matter.

Warwick nimbly scaled the trunk, returning to his perch amongst the sparse foliage. He settled his bony arse into the knotty curve of the branch, confident that the miniature—of stature as well as talent—witchling could not reach the first limb. Clear of the nattering witchling, he silently contemplated his return to the In Between and, from there, back to the Beyond.

His moment of satisfaction was fleeting. She began yapping at him like the horrid, toy-sized canines plaguing this world.

"Settle, little one." He spoke regally as befitted one who once haunted the Goblin King's court. "The night shall fall soon, and we shall part and nere come upon one another, henceforth."

"Lofty talk for a goblin with nowhere to go," she yipped.

Warwick would leave. He, a mighty goblin, could weather this confounded world until the changing of the moon and the return of the Faerie Market. Certainly, he could. He would.

But what would await him at the market?

Would his booth be returned to its original position at the edges of the In Between? Could he proceed as if the night before had not occurred? Or would the darkness swallow him this time instead of spitting him out? He believed it could consume him entirely, as if he had never existed. Or worse, trap him in an existence beneath its depths with the howling mongrels forever more.

A smug auburn fox landed at his side, interrupting his ruminations. The infernal witchling shifted back to her human form, causing the branch to sway and threatening to throw him.

"Don't sit up here and pout. I'm not going to leave you out in the cold. I just need time to explain to my roommate why we have a meddling goblin in our midst."

"Meddling? You, little impudent thief, call me meddling?"

"If the name fits."

A vein pounded against Warwick's temple, threatening to burst, yet she nattered on.

"While we wait, I have a few questions."

Warwick stifled an undignified groan.

"When Fae take humans to the Beyond, aren't they usually trapped until the Fae decide to set them free?"

"Yes," he answered wearily.

"And sometimes they come back different, like kind of messed up in the head."

"As you say."

"So, how does my roommate just come and go as she pleases? You wouldn't think it to look at her, but she is very slippery. My magic slides right off of her."

"Hah." The exclamation of credulity escaped Warwick's throat, unintentionally. "Your magic is frail as gossamer wings. A mewling hatchling could glide through without notice."

Was that a snarl? Though the hairs along his knobby spine rose, he merely shrugged and waited for her to calm herself. He spoke the truth, nothing less.

Her face still sneering in a partial snarl as she asked, "Does that bracelet you gifted her give her some immunity from enchantments?

"Absolutely not. If it had been that valuable, I would not have given it away so lightly."

"That's good, I guess."

"Why?" Warwick asked.

"She lost the bracelet."

Warwick startled and caught himself against the trunk.

"What?" Sabine asked.

"If she has no chain on which to collect the memories, the Fae can, and will, do what they please with her. And their inclinations are not always as fair as their faces."

"Shit!"

Warwick felt in his pocket for the moon charm. It hummed against his fingertips, but he didn't bring it out to show her. She had not asked.

"Aye. Shyte, indeed."

Chapter 13

SABINE

Thunder rumbled from the West. A storm was brewing over the Gulf. Fat raindrops filtered through the sparse tree canopy. A droplet clung to the tip of Warwick's nose, yet he still refused to go inside.

"I'm not so dim as to let a wichling trap me in a house of her choosing."

"Fine. I didn't want to explain why I brought a stray goblin home, anyway." Sabine climbed down, leaving him perched next to the trunk, looking disconcertingly like a knotted branch. "If you catch a cold, don't expect me to magic it away."

The exasperating goblin snorted, sounding like a trumpet through that ponderous nose. "As if I would expect one of your limited abilities to *magic* anything."

The thunder rumbled, closer this time. It rattled the glass in the side door to the cottage. "I'll magic that lightning to strike that limb out from under your bony ass."

Sabine slammed the door behind her and climbed the steep flight of stairs to the attic apartment she shared with Meg. Well, at least when her roommate wasn't off gallivanting with the Fae. Sabine wasn't ready to admit how much it disturbed her thinking of Meg on the other side without the charm bracelet to collect memories or evidence.

The door creaked open behind her.

A deep, rasping voice called, "Sabine?"

She dug in the pockets of her jumper for the key Meg had given her. An effort to domesticate Sabine and get her to use the door instead of the window. Not that her roommate was here to see Sabine using it.

"I thought you were too smart to be caught inside a witchling's home," she called back. The disgruntled goblin could weather the storm outside for all she cared. Only it wasn't the goblin Warwick who stood at the bottom of the stairs. Those warm brown eyes and dark disheveled hair belonged to Jean-Luc.

Detective Thibodeaux flinched as if her sharp words had stung. His 'doing business' scowl settled into place quick enough that she decided she'd imagined the flicker of emotion.

"I need to ask you some questions," he said.

"Ah," she finally found the key in the jumble of clutter in her pockets. "Of course you do. Some magic fuckery erupts and obviously it's my fault."

His jaw tightened. "You were on the scene when I arrived."

Sabine grunted and let herself in as he climbed the steps behind her uninvited. His broad hand stopped the door before she could swing it shut.

"I'm not accusing you of anything. I was hoping you could help."

"And why should I help?"

"People died."

"Died?"

"It's not confirmed, but from eyewitness reports, it would appear several vendors and shoppers were consumed in the blast."

Her stomach roiled at the thought of being devoured by that black maelstrom, but she shrugged it off. Or tried to appear as if she did and glared at his hand holding the door open.

"Not my problem."

Thibodeaux removed his hand, and she started to shut the door when he said, "You came and asked for my help once."

And he had come. He didn't say it, but they both remembered how he faced down a force he barely understood to keep her safe.

Not that he could do much to save her against the magic of the Goblin Market. But he had come. He'd fought to get to her when it was hopeless. And when she emerged with a minotaur at her back, Thibodeaux had stood between her and the raging monster.

Stupid.

Heroic and sweet. But stupid.

"Come in." She left him to shut the door and went to the kitchen. "Coffee? Tea? Whiskey?"

Thibodeaux didn't answer.

Sabine peered around to be sure he'd come in, and she hadn't scared him off like everybody else.

He was there, studying the room with a practiced air. Probably looking for evidence against me, she thought. But knew it for a lie. The furrow between his brows looked more like compassion and curiosity. When he caught her eye, he gave a gentle smile.

Was that pity?

Asshole.

"Coffee. Thanks." Thibodeaux sat on the secondhand couch. Leaning against the cushions, he threw an arm over the back as if this were a casual visit. But his face hadn't gotten the memo. It still wore the detective mask.

Sabine took longer than was necessary, making a mug for each of them from the last two pods Meg had available. Sabine should probably replace them, since she usually drank more than her share while Meg was at work. She made a mental note to lift a box from that chichi shop a block over.

Maybe she shouldn't think such thoughts with a suspicious detective on her couch. Sabine shrugged off the momentary thoughts of contrition. It wasn't really her couch, anyway. Meg bought it to replace the one previously occupied by the dead body of her former roommate.

Handing off Thibodeaux's mug, Sabine curled up in the armchair opposite him, drawing her legs up under her. Thibodeaux sniffed the mug and raised an eyebrow at her.

"French vanilla?"

She offered her mug. "Would you prefer butter toffee?"

He shook his head and took a sip and grimaced at the taste. Leaning forward, he ran a hand through his rain matted hair and wiped it dry on his pants. The furrow dug in deeper on his forehead. He let some of his weariness show through the professional mask.

"You saw what happened at the market," he said, more as a statement than a question.

Sabine sipped her saccharine sweet coffee concoction, buying time to think through her answer. She decided, oddly enough, to go with the truth. Or at least most of it. She'd leave out harboring a runaway goblin.

"I was filling in for Meg at the shop, the Sassy Witch."

Thibodeaux's eyebrow went back up. He was giving it a workout. Jerk. She didn't know if he was skeptical of her working, Meg allowing her in the shop unsupervised, or the name of the shop, which was really no sillier than any other tourist shop in the Quarter.

She narrowed her eyes, and he waved for her to go on.

"The sirens started, and I went to take a look."

"Leaving the shop unattended?" he asked, vaguely amused.

"It's warded," she said defensively.

"Of course it is." After a deep sigh, he settled in to drink his overly sweet coffee and waited for her to continue.

"I could see the black cloud rising before I turned the corner where you saw me. That's as close as I got before I had to get back to the shop." After depositing a goblin refugee in the tree out back.

"The warded magical shop."

"Yes, that one," she said tartly. Did he want her help or not?

But he didn't look as if he were kidding. He set down his mug, rested his elbows on his knees, and clasped his hands as if in prayer. Black tendrils crept across the whites of his eyes, but he looked away before she could get a good look.

Maybe she'd imagined it, but it scared her. She clasped her mug tighter and raised it to hide most of her face. He didn't need to know she'd seen it. But she had.

"Did you," he began haltingly. "Did you see anything in the smoke, other than, well, smoke?"

"Oh," she said, taking a long, slow swallow. "You mean the demons."

Thibodeaux let out a string of curses that had Sabine blushing. She didn't think that was possible. Once he finished, he sat, head thrown back, and stared at the beadboard ceiling as if it might have answers scrawled between the lines in crayon. Or blood.

Could be blood after what had happened here.

"Tell me what you saw inside the market," she said, drawing his attention back to her.

Thibodeaux described the hole in the roof. The crevice in the concrete. The char and the black substance that took a man's arm. The things people saw in the smoke, and those who claimed to see nothing at all. He fiddled nervously with something in his pocket as he related the horrific scene to her.

If he hadn't looked so serious, so bewildered, she might have asked him what he had in there that was so entertaining. But he did. So she didn't.

Shaking his head, he came out of the memory and back to the present to ask, "Can you do something? Anything. Like repair the crevice so nothing else escapes. Or rid the area of that toxic mess before anyone else gets hurt?"

"Not very good at the whole witch thing, remember?" Sabine said. He'd seen how inept she was the night they had fought the River Fae and lost. Thibodeaux'd had bullets and brawn. And she'd had witchcraft so weak, it hardly counted at all.

Running both hands through his hair, standing it up on end, his face twisted with anger at the futility of humans before magic on this scale. "Do you know anyone? Any witches or . . . I don't know, things that counter demons."

"Angels?" Sabine asked. "Not many of those around here, I'm afraid."

But she did know a witch. A sassy, corseted, French floozy of a witch, but strong enough to create the wards on her shop. Something about the spell on the door tickled a memory, but Sabine couldn't quite grasp what it was.

"So what do we do?" Thibodeaux asked, but Sabine wasn't sure he was talking to her anymore. He got up and paced to the window where heavy rain beat against the panes and slid down the glass in rivulets. Thibodeaux's shoulders were tight.

He was a good man. Barely believing in magic, he had to battle against an enemy he did not understand in order to save the people of his city. He took that commitment seriously. Poor, honest, chivalrous soul. She pictured him once again squaring off against that minotour. Thibodeaux would put himself between a monster and those he had sworn to protect.

And he would get himself killed, she thought.

In that instant, she knew what she had to do. Like it or not. She went to stand next to him at the window, looking out on the great oak weathering the storm.

"What the hell is that in your tree?" Thibodeaux asked.

Sabine took a sip of her coffee before answering.

"A goblin. His name is Warwick."

"Of course it is."

Chapter 14

MEGAN

Ice cold light streaked through tall arched openings. Morning had come to this strange land, yet it brought no warmth. Long-limbed creatures, beautiful and horrible to look upon, lined the pale crystal walls. They murmured to one another in guttural voices that Meg couldn't understand.

Predatory eyes tracked her progress across the great hall carved of ice. She could feel their hunger and curiosity press against her flesh, but none moved towards her. At the head of a stone table lounged a monstrous creature, who sat taller than Meg stood. It held up a hand the size of a boulder, keeping the others pinned to the wall.

Further down the table and closer to her sat Baylur, drinking from a silver chalice.

Odd. A fairyland should not be made of nightmares.

Idiot, these are Grimm's tales, not Tinker Bell's.

"My pet," Baylur greeted her as he always did. The longer she stayed in the depth of the castle, the stronger her memories became. This one had become particularly annoying.

"I am no one's pet." She sat at the far end of the table from the great ice giant. The months spent in his kingdom had granted her a fatigue of fear. She could be eaten or beaten at any moment. And there was little she could do to stop it if he allowed it. She didn't know why he held the creatures at bay.

It surely had something to do with Baylur's attention and his relationship with the king. If she broke that bond between her and him or him and the king, what would become of her? But Meg was nearing the end of her patience and, therefore, possibly her life.

She pushed aside a half empty goblet. She'd learned a thing or two during her English studies, thanks to a deviation into the Norse mythology.

Meg leaned back into the oversized chair. In it, her legs dangled like a child playing grownup as she announced, "We have intruded long enough on your Highness's hospitality. Baylur, it's time you showed me the other kingdoms of the Beyond."

A reverberation vibrated up the legs of the chair and into her bones before the sound of rumbling laughter reached her from the far end of the table. The king of the ice giants laughed at her feigned confidence. He winked at her but spoke to the Fae.

"It looks like your human tires of our games. If you have not turned her to you yet, you have failed. Admit your defeat, turn her loose, and pay your debt."

"They all give over in the end," Baylur replied, drinking deeply without taking his eyes from her. The laughter deepened, joined by the cackles and whoops from the perimeter. Meg didn't know if they laughed at the Fae or with him.

A knife the size of a dagger sat beside an enormous platter of steaming meat in front of her. Meg took it up and began to carve into the table. She kept her eyes on both the king and the Fae, who watched her with mild curiosity and seeming disdain.

"Stay," she told the Fae. "Play with the giants." Meg tried to keep her limbs loose and breathe steady. "I'll be exploring the worlds outside this castle. I understand this is one of many on this side of the In Between."

"The only one worth visiting," Baylur said and took another drink, hiding his expression.

Meg wondered if he believed it. Or was he merely flattering the king for favor? Or sucking up out of fear? It didn't matter. She didn't feel such an inclination. Although, seeing the glint in the giant's eye, she might ought to.

"Surely you are right. But how can I judge without checking out the rest?"

A glance down showed that she had scored a steep 'V' in the stone. Maybe it depicted a stubby dagger. The king didn't seem interested in her vandalism. His attention had shifted to Baylur. If that was his real name. She understood names were pretty powerful here. So, she doubted he'd give a real one willingly.

The rumble of the king's voice sent a tremor through her before she could discern the words. "The child does not wish to give you her heart like the rest. Is such a tiny thing so strong? Or are you growing weak?"

The Fae's eyes grew wide and his mouth tightened. Wine sloshed from his chalice, which now bore the imprints of his long fingers indented into the metal. "Toying with the mortals is a fun sport, is it not?"

"It's my heart you're after?" Meg asked. Her chest ached at the thought. She set the blade of the dagger to her chest. The tip cut through her thin sheath, pricking her skin beneath. Warmth trickled around her breast and down her torso.

The sound of animals snuffling filled the room. Baylur's eyes darted to the walls, his lips parted. The king's eyes were latched onto hers. His cheeks rose as a smile crept across his face.

Having caught the complete attention of every creature should have scared her, but instead, it emboldened Meg, who raised her voice so that they could all hear clearly what she had to say. "You think there is a heart here to take?"

Though his expression didn't change, the rise and fall of Baylur's chest gave him away. He, too, panted at the smell of her blood.

"Then come and take it!" Meg threw the dagger down the length of the table. It hit the stone midway and slid until it hit a platter, which held the skeletal remains of a roasted beast.

The muscles in Baylur's arms twitched, but he remained anchored in place. The air grew warmer at her back. Meg feared creatures were closing in behind her and wished very much that she had the dagger back in her hand. The King grunted a command, and the warmth receded.

Shifting his stance, Baylur set his glass on the table. It wobbled on its bent base as he turned a sharp smile on her. "Come, my pet. Upstairs, I will show you adventures you shall never forget within the confines of a single room. We shall find entire worlds to explore inside."

Holding her breath so that it didn't come out in a whoosh of relief, Meg shrugged. Maybe he couldn't take it by force. Or maybe the king wouldn't let him. Baylur collected a handful of spheres from a bowl on the table and pocketed them, and headed her way.

"You'll have to entertain yourself tonight, pet," she told him with a bravado she did not possess. She ran her fingers along the elongated 'V' cut in the stone and stood to leave.

"Go, if you think you can." Baylur waved a dismissive hand toward the door.

Shoulders thrown back, Meg strode to the massive arch at the end of the room. Three horned creatures, vaguely female in appearance, converged upon her. One threaded an arm through Meg's. The creature's horns curled back from behind her ears, down, and around until the tips scraped against her cheeks, leaving rouged abrasions.

"I would be glad to show you the way," the creature said in a voice too rasping to come from those elegant lips.

Another rumble sounded throughout the room.

Meg winced. The king had pounded one monstrous fist upon the table, sending reverberations across the floor. Her female escort darted back to a corner of the room where they cowered.

Baylur's icy eyes were ablaze. The king smirked and tilted his head as if in challenge. And Meg walked from the chamber, having absolutely no idea how to leave the castle, much less the kingdom.

Chapter 15

THIBODEAUX

Jean-Luc refused to stand by and lose anyone else this week. Not on his watch.

As he strode across the patio in the slackening rain, something landed silently at his side. A gnarled man about Sabine's height fell into step next to him. And muttered.

"Witches. They're the worst," the gnarled man said.

Well, he couldn't argue with that.

After a moment's hesitation he couldn't afford, Jean-Luc held out his hand to the strange creature. "Detective Jean-Luc Thibodeaux."

The gnarled man, or goblin, he supposed, looked at Jean-Luc's hand with disdain. "If we're going to work together, you are going to have to stop giving out your name and alliances so easily."

"Fair enough." Jean-Luc withdrew his hand and left, the goblin following in his wake.

With the goblin close on his heels, he explained where he was going and what he intended. The odd creature nodded, as if he already knew. Maybe he did. Perhaps these things were psychic. That might be a problem.

He'd asked him what he intended by coming.

"I need to get from here to the Beyond. And you wish to stop the Beyond from coming here. Our objectives are not unaligned," he'd answered.

Perhaps Warwick could help where Sabine could not.

Warwick refused to ride in the 'sarcophagi of iron' that Jean-Luc had previously thought of as his automobile. The detective explained that cars were made of steel, not pure iron. Warwick gave him the stink-eye and started walking. Even so, the goblin made it to the market first and waited at the edge of the abandoned French Market when Jean-Luc parked.

The market lights lit the underside of the canopy. Jean-Luc had ordered a rotation of officers kept on patrol through the night to be sure no opportunists or homeless or just curious thrill seekers stumbled upon the remains of the tarry substance. The goblin waited outside the pool of light. His shoulders were hunched and his head ducked as if he expected another attack from within the market.

Couldn't blame him for that.

Sabine had given Jean-Luc the rundown of what had happened to the goblin during the explosion, or whatever it was that had happened here. She evaded his question as to why she'd hidden the goblin from him that morning. No one could evade a question like the sly Sabine. He reprimanded himself for thinking of her as dishonest, but that didn't change the truth of it.

"Have you taken a look at the affected area?" Jean-Luc asked.

More stink-eye thrown his way. Looked like the goblin was a regular connoisseur of them. Warwick gestured to the yellow police tape. "A warding circle has been erected around the center."

"Yeah, that. Good call. You're not supposed to cross without a police escort. I just didn't know if you had the same rules over there."

"Wardings apply no matter which side of the In Between you reside," Warwick said, his face twisting with scorn. Or maybe that was its regular shape.

"If you say so. Look, here comes a cop set to patrol the area. I'll talk to him. Just keep quiet, if you would."

Yep, there it was again. That must just be the default setting on the goblin's face.

"Williams," Jean-Luc greeted his fellow officer as he came to see what they were up to. As he watched the man approach, the detective ran through several excuses as to why he had an odd creature like Warwick with him at a crime scene. He hadn't come up with a reasonable one before Williams reached them.

"Detective, what ya got going on?"

"I needed to come back with the crowd out of the way and take another walk of the site," Jean-Luc said. He noticed Willams's eyes slide right over the goblin without stopping.

"It's definitely a strange one. You got any ideas?" William still didn't mention the goblin.

"None that make sense," Jean-Luc hedged, not wanting to get into the peculiar ideas he did have about what happened.

"I got you on that. All's been quiet tonight. Took us most of the evening to send the lookie-loos on their way. Damn tourists will take pictures of anything. But come drinking time and they're off."

"No trouble from the locals, then?"

Williams laughed. "Lord, we seen stranger things come out of the flood waters of Katrina. Nothing here to look at but some burnt tire goo. Or that's what they're saying."

"It's a good enough explanation for the time being." Jean-Luc scratched his chin. His evening stubble had already come in. He swore it sprouted faster every day and itched like the devil. "If you'll keep watch down around the northeast end, I'm going to be up this way for a while. I'll keep watch up here."

"Gotcha. Less walking for me. Not that I don't need it," he laughed again and grabbed his gut with both hands. Jean-Luc laughed with him. "Radio down and let me know when you're headed out and I'll make a full round. Carmichael's replacing me at 3:00 a.m."

Williams waited a beat, checking out Jean-Luc for a reaction. It broke rank for Carmichael to patrol the site when an officer had been assigned. If a replacement was needed, another officer would be sent, not the detective's assistant, unless she or Jean-Luc specifically requested it. And he hadn't.

Jean-Luc almost slipped up and asked what the hell Carmichael thought she was going to do down here without authorization. This was his case, not hers. He knew better than to react like that, but he'd been focused on making excuses for having a goblin at his side. A goblin that Williams didn't seem to notice.

Catching himself short of asking about Carmichael, he said, "Thanks for the heads up."

Williams nodded and headed back to the far end.

Jean-Luc tried to fit together the missing puzzle pieces left around Carmichael. She showed up at the streetcar before he was notified, showed up late to today's scene, and planned to show up here in the wee hours of the morning.

Warwick cleared his throat.

"You will need to lift the ward if you want me to examine the site," the goblin said in the lofty tone usually reserved for New Orleans's old-money families, or newly drunken, self-important visitors.

"Lift the ward. Like this?" Jean-Luc lifted the police tape with one finger, allowing the goblin to walk under. Maybe Warwick didn't want to risk touching it and leaving fingerprint evidence. Or maybe he thought the yellow plastic tape really had magical properties.

Jean-Luc wished the opportunists, the gawkers, and the homeless had an equal level of respect. But if wishes were turds, then here he'd be, he thought. Couldn't be much worse than carved-out bodies and blackened markets with no plausible explanation for either.

Oh, and a witch who couldn't or wouldn't do witchcraft to help. And add a goblin in need of a formal invitation just to take a look.

One thing at a time.

He'd find a way to save the market and find the brutal streetcar killer. He chose this job to save people. If magic invaded his city, he would have to learn to do battle with it.

Empty tables and wire racks threw skeletal shadows across the concrete floor. Jean-Luc and Warwick wove between them. The corrosive tar had receded to a narrow ring thirty to forty feet in diameter, but only a hand's span wide. It no longer appeared to be expanding. Nor was it evaporating. Maybe tomorrow's sunrise would finish it off, if the hole in the roof was big enough to expose the whole ring to the sunlight. If not, Jean-Luc would have roof panels removed and pray the storm clouds moved out.

Inside the ring, the topping had been eaten away from the concrete floor, exposing the gravel inside. It was burned a dark gray. The hole in the center that was exposed earlier in the day was not as large as he had expected.

Jean-Luc's knuckles brushed against the silver pocket watch as he took a coin from his pocket and flipped it onto the concrete within. It struck, bounced once, then rolled to a stop and fell over. It didn't sizzle. It didn't corrode. And nothing materialized to consume it. So, he stretched a hand into the airspace over the circle.

Nothing nipped at him, or caught his hand and dragged him in. Carefully, he stepped over the black ring. Jean-Luc established his footing before bringing the other foot over, so that he didn't slip and fall onto the toxic ring. Two strides took him halfway to the center.

Warwick remained outside the ring, his head turned to the side as if he couldn't stand to look at it

"Is there a problem I should know about?" Jean-Luc asked. None of his nerves bled into his tone, thanks to years of training.

"How can you bear it?" Warwick opened a single eye and was startled to find the detective inside the ring. "Do you not feel it?"

"I can feel the rough floor through the soles of my shoes. It feels cooler inside than out. Should I be worried?"

Warwick cocked his head as if trying to get a different perspective on the evil material. He inched towards it but jerked to a stop.

"It is ghastly. It steals the breath and burns my senses." Warwick's voice had grown raspy.

"Well, back away. Don't let it hurt you." Despite the cool air inside the ring, a bead of sweat slid from Jean-Luc's hairline and into his eye. He wiped it free. "Why isn't it affecting me the same way?"

"You," Warwick spit like a curse, "Are devoid of magic."

"Well, lucky me."

"In this instance, I would have to say you are correct."

The crack in the center of the affected area was about six to seven feet long and eighteen inches wide. He described it to the goblin, including the melted rebar and jagged, blackened edges. The ground underneath looked burnt, but flat. Jean-Luc had expected to find a crevice to Hell. If there had been, it had closed.

"So this toxic sludge broke up through the earth and bubbled out? This other world of yours, the In Between, broke through and spit you out?"

Warwick scoffed. Maybe a sound of pain, more probably one of derision. "The In Between is not under your feet any more than the Beyond is an upside-down version of this realm."

"Of course not." Jean-Luc let the sarcasm seep into his words and was rewarded by a glare from the goblin before he turned his head aside and took another step away. "So where did it bubble up from if not this In Between place?"

"It didn't bubble up. You creatures are so simpleminded."

Jean-Luc's jaw clicked from clenching it. "How about you explain it so that my feeble mind can understand it?"

"I cannot bear it." Warwick groaned.

"Sorry my stupidity is too much for you to stand," Jean-Luc said through gritted teeth.

In answer, Warwick bent in half, gripped his head between gnarled hands, and howled.

"What the Hell?" In two strides, Thibodeaux made it to the edge of the circle headed for the goblin in distress when a wall of black smoke erupted from the ring on the ground, shooting into the air.

Jean-Luc had seen this smoke before. This time, the smoke behind his eyes answered it, roaring in recognition. Taloned hands reached out of the dark mists, grasping for him. Claws hooked into his jacket, pulling him closer.

Fighting desperately, Jean-Luck punched the ephemeral creatures, but his fists met no resistance even as he was dragged in toward mouths, opening and closing. Teeth gnashing. Dark eyes reflecting his own with mists swirling within. And the blackness consumed him.

Chapter 16

SABINE

After Thibodeaux left, Sabine stalked across town in human form to give herself plenty of time to rethink her decision. Yet there she stood, banging on the glass doors of a closed shop in the middle of the night.

The Sassy Witch closed at 10:00 on Fridays, and it was pushing midnight. But Sabine was fairly sure the WITCH of the shop lived in the second-floor apartment. She'd seen Oliver the boy toy coming and going on the back stairs. There was still a light on in the shop. If Georgette didn't open soon, Sabine would consider falling into fox form and finding a way up to the balcony.

"Bébé Sorcière, is that you down there pounding on my door?"

"Yes!" she yelled. That infuriating faux accent rankled Sabine's nerves. Maybe it was a real accent, but Sabine was not prepared to give the witch the benefit of the doubt. She went out to the middle of the street and craned her neck up to catch the silhouette of the woman leaning on the railing above.

Instead of her usual tight pants and even tighter corset, she wore a billowing gown that fluttered around her in the breeze off the river. The apartment lights behind her shone through the gauzy fabric so that anyone passing by would be sure to know that she was naked underneath. Sabine would bet good money—that she didn't have—that that was exactly what the witch hoped.

But the pedestrians tripping back to their hotel rooms from the bars didn't bother to look up, lest they lose their already tenuous balance and fall over. And the guy on the corner asleep under a blanket with his dog curled up next to him probably had seen more than she was offering.

The witch cocked a hip to be sure Sabine took notice, being the only real audience.

"Go home, little girl. We are not open. And your friend is not here."

"My friend?" Sabine asked before she thought better of it. But she'd already started. "What makes you think I am looking for Meg?" How did she know Meg was missing?

"No matter. It is time for *bébé* to be in bed. Shoo-shoo." Georgette flipped a hand at her.

The door opened on the first floor and a sheepish looking young man with a tidy goatee and swoop of hair over one eye came out carrying a shirt and pants draped over his arm. Oliver wore boxers and his shoes were untied. Usually enough for New Orleans, but not in the sometimes cold of February. He darted around the corner, making eyes back at Sabine as if hoping she hadn't noticed him making the walk of shame.

Sabine snorted. Because she was in a foul mood, she yelled loud enough for both Georgette and an embarrassed Oliver to hear, "I see you've already scared your boy toy home to mother. So either come down here, or I'm coming up."

She hadn't figured out exactly how she would get up there yet, but she was resourceful. She'd find a way.

Georgette seemed unperturbed. She leaned both elbows on the railing, her gold bracelet dangling from her wrist. She folded her hands and rested her chin on top to watch Sabine dodge an oncoming car, running without headlights.

After Sabine scampered to the curb and back again, the witch relented. "The door is unlocked if the youngling is gone. Come up and tell Mlle. Georgette how sorry you are for disturbing her evening. And beg for my help."

With that, Georgette went back inside, leaving the French doors open to the cold night air. Sabine opened her mouth to protest that she was not there to beg for anything. Or at least, she hoped it didn't come to that. But she shut her mouth on the reply, just in case she had to do a little begging.

Just a smidgen.

Chapter 17

MEGAN

Crimson droplets struck the bright white snow and bloomed into wine-stained petals. Blood welled along gashes in her arm and ran down her wrists. Wriggling her fingers, she marveled at the color in her palm. She dangled her fingertips over the array of painted poppies growing around her bare feet.

Megan Armand, that was her name. It had taken days to remember. But it was Megan and her friends called her Meg. What friends she had.

What friends did she have?

If they existed, she'd lost their names as well. Their names and faces.

Yet she didn't feel lonely. She didn't feel anything.

She should feel cold, shouldn't she?

Her bare feet had a rosy flush against the snow. They should sting. The cuts down her arms should hurt. Her heart should ache. Yet Meg was numb.

"There you are, my pet." An icy male strode towards her in a stout robe and thick-soled boots. He loomed over her, blue eyes intent. One corner of his mouth twitched before he schooled it into a straight line, then a frown.

Did she know him?

"What are you doing walking the ice flows?" The male ran a hand down her arm and flicked the blood to the side. It splattered against the rock beside a cleft in the stone.

Had she come here to this cave on her own? Why?

"Poor pet. You do not remember, do you?" Baylor said.

Yes, she knew him and his name. He must be a friend. His pale brows pulled together as if worried. Or was he studying her?

Her temples began to throb.

"I've been hunting for you," he said. "You left without telling anyone. You must come back. You were the center of the party. We cannot go on without you."

Meg's vision focused and she could read the look in those eyes. It was hunger. "What do you want from me?"

"What I have always wanted, my pet." His face suddenly very close to hers. His breath striking a freezing line of fire across her cheek and down her neck.

Her feet started to burn, and she stood on first one, then the other, smearing the frozen blood poppies across the snow. "I do not think I have one to give you."

"Everyone has a heart, my pet." He took her arm, his fingers digging into her skin, and led her back toward a crystal palace thrusting up through the ice to pierce the sky.

Meg resisted his pull. "Do you?"

A frozen wind passed over that lovely face, leaving storm clouds behind. The blue eyes turned gray. The bow of his lips became thin and hard. His fingers became claws.

Meg did not cry out. Pain had returned and flooded her body so that the prick of his nails as they sunk into her flesh barely registered. She lifted a hand to his cheek, tracing streaks of crimson along the line of his jaw.

"You cannot hold me here," she said, without passion, neither fear nor anger. "I have no heart to give you. I lost it long ago. You will have to look elsewhere to find one."

Pulling out of his grasp cut fresh lacerations. She felt the burn, but it was nothing compared to the gaping wound left in her chest. Meg had not even known it was there.

Baylor had shown her, though he did not see it himself.

He reminded her of an old and constant ache, even as he took her memories of this place and this time away. No matter. They meant little to her.

She ducked into the dark cave to follow the stream, which bubbled up at the cave's entrance and quickly widened into a rushing current. Behind her, she left the wailing of one who did not get what he wanted for the first time in perhaps a millennium.

A crescent moon reflected deep within the river as it ran through the dark cavern. Meg checked overhead repeatedly to find the stony ceiling intact, no hole through which the moon could peer down into the waters. She didn't understand where the reflection came from, but that was the least of what she didn't know in these strange lands.

The one thing she felt sure about was that she must follow the river. It would lead her to whatever or whomever she had lost. It drew her forward, out of the Fae's spell again.

She hadn't returned so damaged before and wondered what Sabine would say. Her clever roommate would probably berate her for taking off in the first place, or second, or one-hundredth. She couldn't remember the previous visits without the charm bracelet, but Sabine was sure to let her know each and every time.

Maybe it was the thief's way of showing concern.

Or perhaps that was wishful thinking on Meg's part, wanting someone, anyone to care where she went and if she was coming back.

When had she become so needy? So lonely.

Hours passed with only the reflection of the absent moon to light her way through the stone passage. Sabine had explained that time worked differently on this side of the In Between. It worked oddly enough in places like the Midnight Jazz Club, but here, who knew what world she would return to if she ever got out again?

She hoped the New Orleans she left would still be there and not dead and gone, along with everyone she knew.

Imagining she saw a star far ahead, Meg nearly stepped off into the rushing river beside her. Catching her balance, she sank into a crouch to catch her breath. If she'd fallen in, the river would surely have dragged her under to be eaten by some aquatic beast. Or the icy current would simply sweep her away, never to be found again.

The King of the Ice Giants was not here to protect her. Not that he'd cared, she reminded herself. He only wanted to prolong the cat-and-mouse game between her and the cold-hearted Fae.

The star ahead grew until Meg could make out the rough stone edges encircling an opening. So not a star at all, but the bright sky beyond this cave.

Without realizing she'd begun, she ran towards the light and tumbled over a cleft in the rocky floor. She rolled over the edge, barely catching herself before falling headlong into the dark water. The current below caught at her feet and tried to drag her in, but she pulled herself onto the ledge on her elbows.

A slimy body brushed her barefoot before she got herself onto the edge. A long, whip-like whisker felt the air above the water's surface before sinking back beneath. It resurfaced, waved sinuously, then sank, following along beside her toward the opening.

The brilliant sunlight blinded Meg as she stepped from the cave's shadow. Disoriented, she blinked the sunspots from her eyes to find she stood on the Mississippi riverbank at Audubon Park, where she, Sabine, and Detective Thibodeaux had faced down the River Fae, thinking they'd killed Valdi.

They hadn't. She was very much alive and standing at the end of the pier, her back to Meg. Valdi had left her with only a cryptic goodbye before going to study the Fae in their natural, or rather unnatural, habitat. Now, in the dazzling light on the edge of the river, she watched the river rush by as if waiting for something or someone.

Meg stumbled down the pier on bloodied feet. Wet rags hanging from her limbs. A force stronger than the Mississippi drew her to stand beside her former roommate and best friend looking out over the river.

"They said you were looking for me," Valdi said with a lazy smile, still facing the water.

"Was I?" Meg asked, not knowing if it was true or not. "Maybe I was. I was hunting for someone or something I'd lost. Do you have something of mine?"

Valdi turned her face up to the sun and breathed in the loamy air. "The Fae are fascinating, Meg. I could study them for a lifetime and never know all there is to know."

The recent cuts along Meg's forearm seeped blood. It ran down the tip of her fingers and dripped onto the pier. She re-rapped a scrap of linen over the wound, buying time to think why she might be here, now, with Valdi.

"I know they can be dangerous," Meg said. "The one we met at the Midnight Jazz Club came back for me. Over and over, he's come back. I eventually find my way home, but I no longer remember how."

Valdi's eyes lit up with curiosity. "They seek you out? What is it he wants with you, do you think?"

He said I fascinate him, Meg thought. Maybe he is as curious about me as you are about them. Maybe I am alluring, but she knew it for a lie.

"He wants my heart. Wants me to offer it to him. Apparently, he can't just take it." Meg tucked the end of the linen under to keep it in place.

"And you gave it to him?" Valdi was on the track of an interesting cultural tidbit now. Meg could tell by the glint in her old roommate's eye that she'd caught her attention.

"No." Meg sighed and took a step back from the edge of the pier. A step away from Valdi.

"Why not? Weren't you curious what would happen? How it might connect the two of you, maybe make you part of the Beyond." Valdi's expression clouded, as if she were angry or exasperated with Meg for not wanting to know everything like she did.

"I couldn't."

"Why?"

"I didn't have it to give."

Valdi's mouth gaped as if the simple, stupid Meg had said something ridiculous. It didn't hurt. Not too much. Not like it had in the past. Meg shrugged it off.

"So why were you looking for me?" Valdi asked, looking back out to the river, having already lost interest.

"I'm afraid you have something of mine and I need it back."

Chapter 18

SABINE

Usually light on her feet, Sabine trudged up the stairs, weighed down by the rubbish she'd been sent to the shop to retrieve. An amethyst colored crystal tapped at her back. Its chain had somehow gotten turned around on her neck. She held three packs of tarot cards in one hand, the other fist full of an arrangement of herbs. She hugged a grimoire and two blank notebooks to her chest. One had "Double, double toil, and trouble; Fire burn and cauldron bubble," printed on a black cover in metallic letters. The other read "Witch, Please!" She held a crystal ball, free of its box and base, in the crook of the other arm.

One slippered foot caught on a tread midway up the steep stairs. A series of theatrical moves kept Sabine and all the knick-knacks aloft. Steadying herself, she took a cautious step, then another.

"Don't drop the orbuculum," Mlle. Georgette hollered from the top, where she monitored Sabine's ascent.

Sabine felt the reverberation of the witch's voice. Her arm went numb, and no amount of juggling helped. The sphere tipped over her forearm, struck the tread beside her foot, and proceeded to thump against every single step on its way to the bottom. Each strike drove the image of the crystal shattering into Sabine's mind's eye, and she hunched against the inevitable, wondering how many years of bad luck a shattered crystal ball would bring.

It hit the bottom and rolled to a stop in the corner, intact. The fairy lights strung up in the shop filled the crystal with a heaven's worth of stars.

Georgette crossed her arms. "Well, what are you waiting for? Go down and get it."

She couldn't prove it, but Sabine was sure that the witch had caused the tumble. After considering just throwing all the junk to the bottom of the stairs and marching to the top to strangle the witch, Sabine reminded herself that she actually needed Georgette's help.

Like it or not.

And she most definitely did not.

Mumbling under her breath, she went back to retrieve the orb.

Once she'd successfully made it to the witch's apartment above the shop, Sabine dumped her haul onto the antique settee next to her worn satchel and plopped down on a velvet ottoman. Georgette looked way too amused. She still wore the billowing nightgown, but Sabine noticed she was missing the bracelet.

"I assume you have a use for all this junk. Or was this just part of your new witch hazing ritual?"

"There is no such thing as a *new witch*. You are either a *sorcière*, or you are not." Georgette pursed her lips and looked down her pointed nose as she took a sip of herbal tea from a delicate glass with tiny tea roses ringing the rim.

"What a fussy bit—witch." Sabine made the strategic amendment at the last moment, reminding herself again that she needed this woman. Even if it killed them both. And it might.

Out of nowhere, a swarm of wasps swirled around her in a mad, buzzing vortex.

Catching her breath at the sudden attack, Sabine threw up her hands to guard her head, clenching her fingers to keep as much skin from exposure as possible.

The swarm vanished, and she glared at Georgette, who looked askance at her, assessing.

As Sabine spoke, she brushed off her arms to rid her skin of the imagined feel of insects. "Let's get started. And teach me the good stuff. I got bad guys to fight."

That sent Georgette into a fit of laughter that sounded like the shrieking of crows. Faint bird shadows encircled her, and Sabine's face flushed, flaming hot. Acidic words sprang to her tongue, but she fought them down and instead of letting them spew, she slashed a hand through the air to let the witch know enough was enough.

The sound abruptly halted, and the shadows froze, then dissipated. Georgette clasped a hand to her throat, mouth agape.

Sabine tried to offer an innocent smile, but it wouldn't materialize. So, she shrugged instead as the older woman narrowed her eyes and cleared her throat.

"Very well, stand up like a proper lady. Stop slouching about like a street urchin."

Sabine obediently stood. But that didn't stop her attitude from slipping out. "First, we're in New Orleans in the Twenty-first century, not Victorian England. I'm pretty sure they aren't called street urchins. And second, a lady can stand any way she wants. Third, I can't imagine being a lady has much to do with witchcraft, or those hot pants of yours would've strangled every bit of magic out of you by now."

"Oh, *le bébé* is jealous of Mlle. Georgette. Tsk Tsk. We witches must stand together, not put one another down, no matter how scrawny the other might be." She ran her eyes up and down Sabine to indicate which of them was lacking in the curvaceous department.

"Witch," Sabine muttered. Rolling her eyes at the witch's vanity, Sabine happened to catch the flash of gold on the fussy side table. A silk scarf lay on top, hiding it from view, mostly. Was that the bracelet Georgette had worn earlier? Why would she hide it?

The witch began doling out instructions. "Pick up the crystal ball and hold it out to the side. Balance its energy with the crystal necklace in your other hand."

"Really?" One look from the woman and Sabine took off the necklace and turned to pick up the sphere. Stalling for time, while she slipped the gold chain into her pocket, Sabine asked, "Do you expect your boy toy back anytime soon?"

"I fear *mon amour* won't be back. He will be detained."

With her back to the witch, Sabine couldn't see her expression to determine if she was upset about this fact.

"You sound awfully sure," she said, raising the sphere and bracing her elbows against her side. "Did his roving heart slip your clutches?"

Georgette glowered. "His heart is mine. But I've grown weary of it." She smoothed her features. "Extend your arms."

Sabine extended her arms.

"Pull in your core."

Sabine pulled in her core.

Georgette circled her appraisingly. Once around, twice, and the arm supporting the heavy sphere began to tremble. When it dropped several inches, the witch popped her with a magical lash, and Sabine brought it back up, her muscles quivering with the effort.

"Use one to balance the other," Georgette instructed, picking up her teacup and watching her student over the rosy rim.

"How do you do that?" Sabine said through gritted teeth. She was keeping the globe up by tenacity alone.

"Let the energy flow through you, up one arm, down the other."

"Which way?" She asked, as if she knew how to do it either way. "Heavy to light or light to heavy."

"*Question ignorante.* The weight is *insignifiant* to the energy they hold."

"Which," Sabine wheezed. "Has," she gasped. "More."

Georgette tapped a weapon grade metallic nail against her bottom lip.

"Forget it." Sabine dropped the crystal ball on the settee and fell down beside it. She pulled the strap of her satchel over her head. This wasn't going to work. She'd have to figure out how to use magic on her own, and Thibodeaux would just have to wait.

Sucking on her teeth and shaking her head, Georgette pointed her silvered nail at the crystal ball. It rose above Sabine's head, and she flinched. "Go home and put some meat on those scrawny arms of yours. You are hardly fit enough to hold yourself up, much less wield magic."

The sphere came to rest on the top of Sabine's head. Without thinking it through, she swatted it off, sending it flying across the room where it came to a stop, hovering within an inch of Georgette's nose. The witch stared cross-eyed at it.

Sabine hunkered into the settee, awaiting the smackdown that would surely follow. But the delicate corners of Georgette's mouth twitched into a smile.

"So, le *bébé sorcière* thinks she can steal from Mlle. Georgette." She broke out into that cawing laughter.

Crows broke free of her and swarmed Sabine. Beaks aimed for her eyes. Talons raked her cheeks. And, torn from the settee, Sabine flew out the open French doors and into the night.

Chapter 19

WARWICK

As Warwick watched Detective Thibodeaux, a haze coalesced above the blackened ring. It shimmered, then turned hungry eyes on the goblin. Teeth snapped in his direction. Dark spirits beckoned him. Later, he would be loath to admit that he might have answered them if the detective had not, at that moment, come blundering out of the circle, bellowing and punching at unseen enemies.

Detective Thibodeaux roared like a rampaging rhinoceros bull. He swung a fist into the black mist. It met no resistance, and he stumbled out of the ring, falling to a knee. A stretch of bare flesh below the leg of his trousers touched the ring and sizzled. If Warwick had not stepped in to aid him, the poor sodden man would surely have lost the leg, along with his sanity.

Fortunately, due to his stalwart manner, Warwick overcame his repulsion to the black magic, dragged the detective clear of the circle, and wrapped the wound in a pocket kerchief. A well-used one, regrettably, but one must use what one has at hand.

The man, Officer Williams, came running at the sound of his leader's distress. Warwick quickly covered the bandage with the detective's pant leg and stepped aside. There was nothing for it but to let this human see him.

"Thibodeaux, you okay?" the man asked as the detective pushed himself to a stand, rubbed a hand across his eyes, and shook his head as if dazed.

Warwick answered for him. "I came upon this gentleman as he stumbled from that hideous circle. The fumes must have overwhelmed him, but he seems to have caught his bearings."

The officer's hand made a warding gesture toward the black ring to fend off evil. He met the detective's eye, then nodded his thanks to the goblin. The simple human officer did not see a goblin before him, or his mind refused to do so. The man mistook Warwick for a human. Which he chose to take as a compliment to his glamour and not as an insult.

"Is there someplace close by that we might get this man some libations until he can clear his head?" Warwick asked and took the detective's elbow in hand.

"I . . . uh, sure. The Priory's just over here." The man called headquarters, then led the glamoured goblin and his dazed superior to a pub on the row between the market and the rest of New Orleans.

The dim lights of The Priory made it easy for Warwick to keep his glamour in place. He nearly blended in with the dark wood-paneled walls and bench. Yet if eyes landed directly upon him, he would appear as a rather short man with a rather large nose and ears. He led the detective to a table in the back corner, past the bar and its string of yammering humans.

Williams waved them on and remained at the bar to order a round. Quickly enough, he returned with two glasses and handed one to Warwick and one to Thibodeaux. Whiskey, he called it. A weak brew but serviceable to pass the time as the portly human officer coaxed his commander to take a drink.

"A slug of that'll bring Thibodeaux back to his senses," the officer assured Warwick, then encouraged the detective. "Have a drink. It'll fend off the fumes of that cursed place."

Warwick sipped at the weak spirits as he kept an eye on the detective. The inky mists still swirled behind Detective Thibodeaux's eyes. He drained his glass in one long swallow and slammed it onto the scarred wooden table. While Williams went back to the bar for another, Warwick unwrapped the detective's wound and doused it with his own drink. It washed away most of the remaining contaminant. Warwick had been loath to touch it himself, lest he be infected and therefore no use at all to the human. He wiped his hands on his britches at the thought.

The detective's leg most probably would heal in time. His sanity less probably. Warwick thought it best not to share this too readily with the extra human returning to hover like an overly protective hen.

"You got him?" he asked Warwick, who gave a jerk of his head. "Thanks, I got to get back to my post. You sure he'll be okay, right?"

How should Warwick know?

He grunted in response.

"Thanks, man. I'll take care of this round. Thibodeaux might need another before he feels like himself. Can you cover it?"

Warwick held up a finger.

"Good. Good. Thanks, again." With that, he hustled out of the pub.

Thibodeaux's head lolled about his shoulders drunkenly. His pupils dilated, then constricted. The dark magic inside them seemed to catch sight of Warwick and flared before receding.

"You," the detective slurred.

"Yep, me."

"What the hell was that? It attacked me just like before."

Warwick choked on the mouthful of liquor. He struggled to swallow before carefully setting his glass in the center of the disc provided to absorb condensation. "You've met this magic before?"

"It's in me. I can feel it growing." The detective leaned in conspiratorially. "You can see it in there. Can't you?"

Warwick grunted.

The detective swore as if the goblin's response had been confirmation.

Warwick should not be surprised that these simple creatures communicate in remedial sounds. He studied the water droplets lining the sides of his glass, reflecting the amber whiskey, before speaking, "Describe exactly the moment this magic attacked you the first time."

And the detective did. It took him another visit to the bar and another round of whiskey to give the full account. When he had finished, they sat silently mulling over their empty glasses.

Thibodeaux jerked into full recognition and propped a leg onto the chair. He jerked up his pant leg and ripped off the bandage Warwick had hastily applied. They were both aghast at the sight.

The pulped, weeping wound had closed. A layer of black, ragged skin had formed over the flesh that had been eaten away by the magic sludge.

"I saw it eat a man's arm off. It was eating at me, too. You stopped it with your magic," Thibodeaux accused the goblin.

"I *am* magic. I do not *do* magic." He spat back at the ungrateful mortal. "It's your magic fighting back to keep you whole."

"I have no magic."

"You do now."

"That thing growing in me. *It's* magic. Not *me*."

"Most probably. But what difference is there while it resides in you?"

"Can it control me?"

"Not yet, it would seem." How was he expected to have all the answers? Although compared to them, he must seem all-knowing.

"You *do* conjure magic. This." Thibodeaux jerked a silver pocket watch from his pants pocket and smacked it onto the tabletop hard enough to crack the crystal face. "You did this. You enchanted it. Sabine said it was a goblin, like you. You are the vendor from the other market."

"I sold it. I did not make it."

"How did you get here from there?"

"The heart of the market swallowed me, then spit me out."

"Why?"

"As punishment, I assume."

"For what?"

"I do not answer to humans." How dare he show such insolence as to question one who once served at the pleasure of the Goblin King?

This human knows nothing of the Goblin Court, he told himself. And though he had known it before, still the realization hit him hard. He might be banished to these lands forever amongst ignorant souls who knew nothing of the beauty of the Beyond. His hand began to tremble, and he clutched his glass to still it. The detective did not seem to notice.

Thibodeaux's eyes shone bright and feverish. He pointed at the pocket watch. "Can you reprogram it? Could we use it to trap this substance like it trapped me? Make the market safe for people?"

"It was not made to trap a place, but a person. Only the owner can reprogram it."

"I am the owner now."

"Then you can set it to trigger upon whomever you please," Warwick said sourly.

"Who would I trap to keep this evil from getting into New Orleans?"

Warwick was sickened to see this honorable man wishing ill on another. "You would visit that horror on someone else?"

"To trap a killer and save people, I would."

"Ah, so you are a judge and executioner now?" Warwick cocked an eyebrow.

"You *sold* it *knowing* what it was for," the detective spat back at him.

And that was the truth of it. Warwick deserved his banishment. But he was not willing to be put in place by this meager human whom he had just saved.

"You keep this trinket," he flicked his hand toward the timepiece. "Which traps a body inside a time and place? That is why your hand strayed to your pocket time and again. And yet, you would fault me for trafficking in black magic goods, yet you're loath to let go of it."

That set the human back a moment. Detective Thibodeaux studied the watch as if it might turn on him again. Neither of them spoke as they drained their second glasses of whiskey. Thibodeaux picked up the silver pocket watch, put it back in his pocket, and returned his hands to the tabletop before speaking.

"And what is it you keep in *your* pocket?"

Warwick had not noticed that his fingers were again caressing the moon charm brought to him by the witchling's familiar. After considering a denial, he brought forth the golden crescent moon and laid it beside his glass.

"That from the infamous charm bracelet?"

"It is."

"And you're behind that as well."

"I gifted the lady the chain only. It requires each creature she meets to provide a charm. These hold a memory of their interaction. Otherwise, a human will lose all recollection. A simple but effective way to hold creatures to task for their behavior."

"Well," Thibodeaux asked, "What memory does it hold?"

"I don't know. It is not my memory. But I fear it is important. The witchling's familiar, the crow brought it to me in exchange for its voice."

The detective scowled. Warwick was learning this meant he was puzzling through the bits and pieces of information he had collected thus far. He gave the human space to process. He had no need to chatter like the humans he had come into contact with. And appreciated that the detective did not seem to need to either.

At last, the detective nodded, apparently to the picture forming in his mind's eye, then addressed Warwick. "We must go see the lady who can read it."

"Not all things are meant for you to know."

"If it concerns my people, the people of New Orleans, then it is meant for me."

A noble if foolish sentiment.

"If she has returned from the Beyond," Warwick said as he rose and motioned for the hobbled detective to take the lead.

Chapter 20

SABINE

That scrawny Georgette had actually thrown Sabine off her balcony.

The witch!

Well, it was more like levitating, or some other such magic BS. Sabine freaked out and caught herself mid-air. Sprawled out, arms and legs waving helplessly, Sabine grabbed for her satchel as it slipped off her shoulder. She caught her breath, glanced over her shoulder, then slowly sank to the asphalt in the middle of the intersection.

A horn blared as a dark Subaru screeched to a halt at the stop sign. Sabine flipped it off. It should've stopped, anyway.

"*Toi, voleur,*" Georgette spit the accusation over the balcony. To be sure Sabine understood, she repeated it in English. "Thief. Come back here, or I will hunt you down and tear the skin from your carcass, strip by strip."

Sabine did not wait around to see if the witch was true to her word. Fearing that line of sight might be important in casting skin rending spells, she ducked under the closest balcony, fell into fox form, and ran. Her satchel thumped against her haunches as another car squealed through the intersection.

Tongue lolling out of her snout, Sabine wove a circuitous route through the streets of New Orleans to be sure the witch was not on her tail. Reaching the tree behind the cottage where she stayed with Meg, Sabine sprang into its canopy. To her relief, the goblin was gone. She'd consider where he might have gone after she was safe from Georgette's wrath.

The bedroom window, which she was sure she'd left open, was closed. She yipped and barked to get her roommate's attention before remembering Meg had not come home in nearly a week. In her panic, she'd forgotten her anxiety over Meg possibly being trapped on the other side.

As Sabine cursed herself for having closed the window, a shadowy figure stumbled up to the glass, pushed the curtain aside, and raised the window. The shadow moved back, and Sabine made a practiced leap.

Inside, the shadowy figure revealed itself to be a bedraggled Meg. Without speaking, her roommate left Sabine panting in the middle of the floor as she staggered into the living room and tumbled onto the couch. Locking the window, Sabine followed, only to stumble to a stop in the doorway.

Meg sprawled with one arm across her forehead. Her hand clutched her chest. Stained strips of cloth encircled both forearms. Her face was pinched in pain. Her hair was matted. Her feet were bare, blistered, and splattered with dried blood.

"What happened to you?"

"Can we not talk about it?"

Checking that the door was locked, as if that would keep creatures or enraged witches out, Sabine considered the request. "For now. But don't think we're not circling back around to that. You were gone a long time. I thought I might have to go in after you."

Meg eyed her from under her arm. "You think that's wise? No magic and all."

"I've got magic."

"Right." Meg closed her eyes.

"I went to ask Madame Witchy Pants to teach me."

Meg's brows rose, but her eyes stayed shut.

"I know. Stupid move. But I was getting a little desperate. I needed all the artillery I could get if I was going to snatch you out of the clutches of the Fae. Plus, Thibodeaux needed my help." She added the last, too quiet for Meg to catch.

Taking a shaky breath, Meg asked, "How long was I gone?"

"Days."

"That's not too bad."

"It is if you're trapped in the Beyond."

"In the Beyond, it was months."

Months? Sabine didn't know how to respond to that. Meg had been with the Fae, or who knew what else, for months and returned in wrapped bloody bandages. This could not be good.

"How did you get out?"

"I walked."

"You don't just walk out of the Beyond. Once the Fae have someone, they don't just leave. Except you do, I guess." Only this time, it didn't look as if they'd let her go willingly. "Did you fight your way through a legion of trolls on the way?" She folded herself into the armchair to examine her roommate.

Meg flipped a hand to dismiss Sabine's skepticism. "No bracelet, remember."

"Oh. Right. Here." Sabine dug in her jumper pocket and pulled out a gold chain adorned with several charms: silver, gold, carved stone, and jewels. Letting it dangle from her finger, she waggled her eyebrows at Meg. "Pretty slick. Right?"

Meg sat bolt upright. "Where did you get that?"

"Mlle. Fancy Faux Witch herself, Georgette," she said triumphantly. "Only she might be a real witch and just faux French."

After a moment's thought, she added, "She might actually be French, too."

Meg started pacing across the small living room, dodging furniture as she went. She snatched the bracelet from Sabine's hand on her second pass by. "First of all, how did Georgette get it? Second of all, you stole from her? Are you an idiot? She'll hunt you down and skin you alive."

"Those were her exact words, actually, along with some additional rather graphic threats."

Meg flopped back onto the couch. "Shit."

"Yep."

Crimson streaks seeped through the bandages on Meg's arms.

"Look, do you need to go to the doctor? You don't look so good."

"It's just my heart."

"You're making my point."

"No, it's working okay. It's just killing me. You know how you don't know how painful it can be? When you've lost it, I mean. It's not until you get it back broken that you realize what a pain it is to have one." Meg pressed a fist into her chest as if the organ might burst through.

"Sure," Sabine mumbled, then thought it through. Trying to give an honest answer for once, she amended her response. "No, I don't know that."

"Because you haven't gotten yours back," her roommate said, a statement rather than a question.

"Or I never lost it. I don't just leave it lying around for anyone to pick up." Sabine's tone surprised her. It sounded like she meant to hurt Meg, who was already in pain. She opened her mouth to soften the blow when Meg spoke.

"Hmmm, poor you."

"What the hell? Do you like pain?" Sabine demanded. Meg's mind was obviously scrambled from her time on the other side. She didn't answer. She just lay there looking miserable.

With an effort, Sabine gentled her voice. "Broken hearts suck. But you got it back. That's good, right?"

Meg's eyes were screwed shut. "I didn't know it could hurt this bad."

"I'm sorry about the heartache and all that happened to you over there. We can talk about it when you're ready."

Meg sighed.

Sabine added in a near whisper, "I'm glad you're back."

Meg dropped her hand and squinted at Sabine. "You were really going to go in after me?"

"What did you expect me to do? Wait forever for you to get back? The rent is due soon." It wasn't a nice thing to say, but it made Meg snort. So, it was a win of sorts. Sabine couldn't articulate the ugly feeling of pent up fear that had grown in her roommate's absence. Fear *for* her, and also loneliness *without* her. Neither pretty emotions.

"Thanks."

"Keep your thanks. I didn't get there, did I? And you come home looking like you mistook a cheese grater for a luffa."

"She's a real witch then, Georgette?"

"I suppose. Fat lot of good it did me. She's more into torment than teaching."

"She's going to come after you. You know that, right?"

"Yeah. I better leave for a while. Lie low."

"That's fine. I should've moved out of this place a long time ago."

"Why?" Sabine asked. "I mean, yeah, sure. The witchy woman might come for the both of us. You and me. Sorry about that."

Meg shook her head.

"You've got a reason other than being jointly skinned alive?" Sabine asked.

"This is Valdi's apartment. Mine and Valdi's."

"Oh, so I'm just a squatter here. Is that what you're saying?"

"I'm saying this place has old intentions that don't fit my current reality."

"Oh." What else was there to say?

"So, your aunt's house, then?" Meg asked, as if it were that simple.

"Blood all over the floor. Holes in the walls. Bad vibes. Remember?"

"Right now, my shitty vibes beat yours."

"How's that?"

"Because mine are newer."

How do you argue with that? As far as timelines go, Meg was right. Sabine could argue that death was more permanent than heartbreak, but she wasn't sure that was true.

Sabine headed to the bedroom. "You rest. I'll pack, then we'll go see how big a mess my aunt's house is."

"We need to move fast, huh?" Meg mumbled, throwing her arm back over her eyes.

"I didn't have time to look back, but I'm pretty sure those were fireballs Georgette was throwing at me," Sabine said, stuffing clothes into an empty shopping bag.

Chapter 21

THIBODEAUX

The wound on his leg had healed with astonishing speed, but it hurt like the devil. Jean-Luc wasn't sure that it wasn't the devil himself who'd gnawed a hole in his calf. The blackened scar sure looked demon made. He drove to the cottage where Sabine now lived in Megan Armand's attic apartment. The door to the stairs was locked, and he didn't have a number to call.

Why would he? Sabine probably didn't even own a phone. But Megan Armand would.

The department would have it. He might be able to go by before the first shift came in. Before Carmichael showed up to ask why Jean-Luc looked like he'd been dragged through the streets.

"They are not here." The goblin's voice startled him. Jean-Luc half expected the creature to be at the house when he pulled up, but he hadn't seen him when he arrived nor heard him approach.

"How do you know?"

"The tree told me."

Jean-Luc opened his mouth to ask what that meant, the ingrained habit of a detective gathering information. In this case, he knew it would not help, so he shut it. A young man in khakis and a pale blue button-down, complete with a neatly folded pocket square, came out the front door.

"You looking for the upstairs duo?" the young man asked. "They're an odd pair, right? Can't tell if they're a couple or just, you know, splitting the rent."

"They don't appear to be home. Do you have a number for either of the women?" Jean-Luc asked as the man walked past him and the goblin on the way to a nondescript sedan. He didn't seem disturbed by Warwick. He didn't seem to notice the goblin at all, even though they were less than an arm's length apart.

"Naw. I think they're gone. Moved."

"You wouldn't know where they might have moved, would you?" he asked with little hope.

"I've barely spoken to either of them. Sounded like they were moving out. Lot of banging cabinets, drawers, doors. Saw them carting boxes out to the tall one's car a couple of hours ago. Probably skipping out on the rent."

Jean-Luc cursed, which wasn't professional of him. He wasn't on the clock, but that had never mattered before. He tried to always behave as if he were representing the NOPD even when he wasn't.

The young man cocked his head, giving Jean-Luc a sympathetic half-smile. "One of them an Ex? Steal your stuff? Happened to me. Girls are such—"

"Thank you for your help," Jean-Luc cut him off.

"Look, if it helps, my girlfriend saw the tall one working at that Voodoo shop about a block away from the French Market."

"Thanks." That covered half the tourist shops, but it was a start.

The lights on the young man's car blinked and his horn bleated as he unlocked the sedan. He stepped into the car but stopped before sitting and called over the door. "Brassy Witch. That's the name of the shop. Or something like that. Maybe Cheeky or Cocky Wizards shop. You know, something like that. That help?"

"Yes," Jean-Luc said, although it didn't.

"The Sassy Witch," Warwick murmured.

"What was that?" the guy asked, door nearly closed.

"Sassy Witch?" Jean-Luc asked.

"Yeah! That's it! Katy loves that shop. Crappy witchy shit. She eats it up," he said as he slammed the door.

"If the witch who owns it heard him, he be eating her feces," Warwick muttered.

Jean-Luc choked back a laugh. "Right. You know where it is?" The goblin nodded. "I'm driving. I assume you're walking or whatever it is you do?" He needn't have bothered asking. The goblin had already disappeared into the early morning shadows.

Punching the shop name into his GPS, Jean-Luc headed over to see what a sassy witch's shop looked like. And hoped to find Meg without Sabine in tow. Although he couldn't say why.

"That stretched piece of useless human flesh is no longer employed here," the owner told him. Jean-Luc could not tell if she was a real witch or not, but she certainly dressed for the part in her 'sexy witch' Halloween costume. She didn't bat a fake eyelash at his derelict state, so he shouldn't judge her choice of attire.

"Thank you, ma'am." Jean-Luc headed for the door. Warwick waited outside.

"Not inclined to enter the establishments of witches," he'd said.

Jean-Luc opened the door, and the bell jangled overhead.

"Wait, *monsieur*. You are a detective. I have a complaint to file regarding that *voleur de miniatures* who plays nursemaid to Mlle. Megan."

Jean-Luc understood enough of the Cajun French to gather that he did not want to hear what the woman had to say about the 'mini-thief.' Even though he had a hard time imagining Sabine as anyone's nursemaid, she most definitely fit with the rest of the description.

If the shop owner filed a complaint, he would finally have to address Sabine's lawless nature. About time, he told himself, and pulled out the pad he kept in his jacket pocket.

"What is it she stole?" he asked, knowing it was something.

He gave the shop a look over to see if Sabine could have tucked enough merchandise into that satchel of hers to constitute a felony or just a misdemeanor. Practicality said the latter, but he knew the sneak thief to be very crafty. Who knew what she got away with this time?

"My magic," the Mlle. Georgette proclaimed.

Jean-Luc's pencil hovered over the pad. The goblin peeked through the window, agape. He must have overheard. Jean-Luc took a deep breath, closed his pad, and put it back in his pocket. "I think we're going to need to sit and have a talk."

The woman had the nerve to smirk. There was absolutely nothing funny about this.

A half hour later, he rose to leave with a full report of all the spells Sabine had supposedly stolen. He didn't doubt she did it. Not anymore. But there was no way to file a proper report about that.

Mlle. Georgette put a hand on his arm, wrapping spike-like silver nails around his wrist. They met on the opposite side, clinking like knife blades. "*Un de plus*, Detective. I must also tell you of my poor missing shop boy."

Letting loose an exasperated sigh, he sat again to hear about the latest missing person. Although Georgette seemed enthusiastic while telling him about the young man, she seemed much less concerned over 'the shop boy' disappearing than she had been over Sabine's thievery.

What concerned Jean-Luc was how accurately the description of this man fit that of the streetcar victim. And the missing man from last fall, Jean-Luc thought, but shoved it aside. That man was supposedly accounted for, although not to Jean-Luc's satisfaction.

"When did you last see him?"

"Last night when he left my *boudoir*."

"Your *boudoir*?" Jean-Luc wrote 'bedroom,' before looking up from his notes. "Ma'am, if he left your apartment only last night, what makes you think he is missing? Have you tried calling him?"

"He would not answer if I did." She appeared rather smug for someone reporting a missing person.

Jean-Luc assumed this was a relationship issue, which he did not have time to deal with. Or the witch had simply scared the man senseless with those long silver nails of hers. Maybe he knew better than to answer this woman's call.

She put that theory to rest.

"He would not answer, because he has been stolen from me." Her eyes sparkled, literally. Which was unnerving. And she smiled, obviously enjoying this charade.

"By whom?" Jean-Luc asked patiently, while considering how to extricate himself from this conversation.

She looked coy. "The Fae."

She cocked her head as if waiting for him to protest, but he did not have the time.

"Of course," he said, shutting the notepad once again. She seemed disappointed by his reaction. "Why do you believe a fairy stole him?"

"Not a fairy, *stupide*."

Jean-Luc did not need his limited understanding of French to catch that one. He stood to leave. "Ma'am, the NOPD does not have jurisdiction over Fairyland."

"But you do look after humans, *n'est pas*?"

"*Oui*," he said and sat back down.

Chapter 22

MEGAN

Green ferns sprawled out of their pots. The tip of each frond dripped from last night's rain onto the newly refinished deck below. Clear glass winked in the shifting shadows cast by the early morning sun. The front door and shutters wore a fresh coat of eggplant colored paint.

"I don't see what's wrong with it."

"It's creepy," Sabine said sullenly.

"What's wrong with you?" Meg asked. Sabine's face twisted. She had described her aunt's house as an abandoned building staring out with dead eyes. Meg wouldn't have suggested coming here if staying hadn't been too dangerous. But the cottage looked well cared for. "It's perfectly charming. Does pleasantness cause you actual pain?"

"We should go around back and peek in the windows."

"Don't you have a key?"

"Yes, but we can't just walk in. Look at it."

Meg looked down at the strange little witch next to her, crouching behind a car on the far side of the street from the cottage. "You don't have the key, do you?"

"I said I did."

"Show it to me."

Sabine dug in the pocket of her jumper. Meg marveled at how many different pockets and pouches the woman carried on her person and how much stuff she could secret away inside them. Holding out a copper-colored key balanced on her palm, Sabine gave her a smug expression, or rather she wore her normal face, which was nearly always smug.

"Great," Meg said, swiping the key before Sabine could close her fist around it, and stalked across the street. Sabine hopped up and chased after her.

"Someone's been here. Recently."

"To water the plants. Oooohhh, very creepy." Meg marched up the steps to the porch, dodging a seeking frond from the closest fern. It dripped onto her shoulder despite her dodging and ran down her arm. She wiped it across her T-shirt and tried the key in the lock, assuming it would have been changed.

Sabine moved silently along the porch to peer through the windows. "Maybe the city reclaimed it and sold it to someone." She had an odd lilt to her voice, between hopeful and wistful.

The lock clicked, and Meg's hand froze. Sabine was instantly at her side, staring at the knob as if it might bite. She bounced on the balls of her feet as Meg turned it and the door opened with a sigh.

Inside, the verdant light filtered in from the porch to show an eclectic, yet tidy, living room. The air had the mild stale odor of rooms left empty too long. Meg flipped the switch by the door and the ceiling fan stirred the air, lifting the heavy feeling. She reached for the pull cord to turn on the fan's light, but Sabine caught her arm and shook her head.

She was such a suspicious creature. Not that Meg could blame her. A touch of that suspicious nature might have saved

Meg from her chilling days spent in the Beyond. But everything was so warm and colorful and normal in this house that she could not help but feel at home, despite having no connection to Sabine's aunt.

Sabine, her arms crossed and her back to the door, surveyed the room warily.

"If I can face Valdi, you can face a kitchen." Meg headed to the narrow hallway.

"There's a big difference," Sabine said without budging from her spot.

"You don't say." Meg rubbed at her sternum, unable to ease the ache.

"You knew Valdi was alive," Sabine said, pushing off the door and shoving past Meg. "And I know my aunt is dead."

"It's easier to mourn them when they're dead," Meg muttered.

Windows lit the small kitchen. Its walls were a vibrant, if startling, yellow, with avocado green cabinets. A long wooden table covered with a floral plastic tablecloth sat in the middle, and a wood frame hung over it, with over a dozen metal hooks dangling, empty.

Sabine dropped to the floor and started crawling around on hands and knees, her face inches from the floorboards.

"Uhm, you forgot to shift. You're still human," Meg told her.

"It's gone."

"The body?"

"The blood." Sabine's nose twitched unnervingly like a canine.

"Are you a hundred percent sure you're not a werewolf, or whatever you call a fox person?"

"A shifter," Sabine said, popping up to her feet. She began making a close inspection of the sink and countertops. "And don't say that again or they'll come after the both of us. Shifters are very proud and don't like the fact that I can shift. They call it stealing."

"Well, you are a thief." Meg gave her a very Sabine-esque shrug when the witch glared.

Instead of barking at her, though, Sabine pointed to the cabinets accusingly. "They painted it."

"Who?"

"How should I know? But somebody has been here, scrubbed and bleached the floors, and repainted the whole room."

Meg laughed. "That's good to know. I'd hate to think your aunt's color sense was this tacky."

"They repainted it the same color. She picked it out years ago."

"Oh."

Sabine opened and closed every cabinet door and every drawer. "Can't you smell it? It's fresh paint, just like the front door."

"It's not sticky," Meg said, touching the startlingly yellow wooden wall panel.

"Not that fresh."

"So, someone did move in and repainted it the same exact color?" That two people would choose this same combination was unthinkable.

"No. The dishes, the potholders, and towels. All that stuff is my aunt's, but not the new cleaning supplies under the sink." Sabine looked stunned, almost as if she were seeing the bloodstains for the first time instead of fresh paint and scrubbed floors. "Maybe the police had it cleaned and painted after their investigation."

"They don't do that," Meg said, remembering her landlord complaining about the cost of the cleanup after Valdi's supposed murder. While Meg relived the gruesome scene, something happened that she would never have imagined in a thousand years.

Sabine was crying. Fat tears rolled down her cheeks and her chest hitched as a sob broke loose.

Meg crept up to Sabine like one does a wounded yet dangerous animal and wrapped her arms around the prickly woman, hoping she wouldn't bite.

She didn't.

Light shimmered off the bottom of a copper pan hanging on the wall, sending shimmering sparks through Meg's vision as the petite witch clung to her. Meg clung back. Both of them wretched and alone. But together.

Chapter 23

WARWICK

After the detective finished his inquisition of the wretched witch woman, Mlle. Georgette, Thibodeaux described the spot on the river where he planned to look for a 'stolen boy.' He offered to escort Warwick to the docks. Of course, Warwick refused to enter the man's metal carriage he called a car. The goblin made faster time on his own and met the detective at a large structure, also made of metal.

"Are you coming in, or do you need to stay outside?" Detective Thibodeaux asked.

Warwick surmised that the interior was big enough that he probably would not fall ill from iron sickness. Without answering the detective, he stepped over the threshold.

Inside, magnificent creatures, taller than ice giants, loomed over the space lit by atrocious lanterns pulsing with electricity, as if a thousand faeflies were imprisoned in each one. The glare pierced Warwick's vision, causing it to waver. Creatures perched atop large rolling wagons, seeming to vibrate while humans swarmed around them, erratic servants to their betters.

Creatures this grotesque, this monstrous, and this majestic did not exist on this side of the In Between. Warwick lifted his hands to feel for any magic that might allow these creatures passage from the Beyond. Yet the air slipped between his fingers, useless and bereft of magic.

Once his eyes adjusted, the creatures no longer moved. They stood sentry, silent and lifeless. Only statues. At the far end of the space, infernal machines buzzed like maddened hornets as their human counterparts carved the face of a long-dormant god. Warwick had thought him to be lost and forgotten.

"Who worships these innocuous effigies?" Warwick asked. The detective prowled around the end of a carriage he called a parade float without answering. Whimsical depictions of fearsome beasts lined the perimeter. If the actual beings from the Beyond saw themselves reproduced by these clumsy humans, blood would coat the dusted floor of the warehouse.

An artist halted her work as Thibodeaux approached her. "Detective Thibodeaux with the New Orleans Police Department," he said. "Are you on the krewe of the Eros float?"

"Yes, and we're behind." She cleaned her brush and reloaded it with paint as she spoke. "I need to get back to it. Have to repair these scuffs some idiots cut across the paint last night. I have to finish today so the paint sets before the parade. What is it you need?"

"I understand that someone named Oliver worked on your krewe. Is that correct?"

The artist sneered. "Oliver signed on and came to drink and distract the whole krewe. If you call that work, then yeah. Although he didn't even bother showing up tonight. Good thing. We don't have time to waste on that playboy."

Thibodeaux showed the woman a picture to confirm the identity. "Is it unusual for him to miss a night?"

"Actually, yes. That was the only reliable thing about him. He showed up right after work. Supposedly, he was a clerk at that shop in the Quarter. Bet he didn't do anything worth a damn there, either." She bent back, carefully painting away the mar down the side of the float. "Why? Something happen to him? Did he get in some trouble? Messing with the wrong crowd?"

"Did you know him to mess with the wrong sort?" Thibodeaux asked, and Warwick left him to his inquisition and circled the wagon. He had no interest in one errant human.

The fact that this trivial distraction caught the detective's attention irritated the goblin. At the human market and later in the pub, the detective had proved himself to be a man of some intelligence. Then Warwick had observed Thibodeaux through the window as he quizzed the inept witch, Mlle. Georgette. From these interactions, Warwick had felt certain the inquisitive detective could be of use to him, though he offered his name too willingly.

Detective Thibodeaux saw magic for what it was. Although those dark shadows behind his eyes concerned Warwick, he could overlook the contamination as long as the man kept his wits and will about him. Walking into this edifice dedicated to the worship of gods and creatures, old and new, known and unknown, indicated Thibodeaux had a healthy respect for the world beyond.

Yet, again, the man was distracted by the weak and pointless humans. Perhaps he feared the wrath of the formidable witch known as Mlle. Georgette. Warwick had smelled the darkness on her, so pungent that he could not enter her abode, though he worried over the detective. Humans came and went from the establishment, relatively unharmed. Warwick protested, but ultimately let the detective enter.

As he pondered the easy distractibility of the seemingly alert detective, Warwick clambered onto the wagon. He hoisted himself up onto the wheel and grasped the rail above. Green lightning arced off the metal, and Warwick was thrown to the wall.

He tumbled mid-air to strike with his shoulder instead of his head and fell to the floor, where he rolled onto his feet. Landing in a fighting stance, he surveyed the enormous sculptures towering over him for signs of life. Nothing breathed. Not a one moved. No eye flickered his way.

Thibodeaux had withdrawn his tablet and scribbled inside it, unaware of what had happened. The artist had returned to her work, continuing to answer his questions.

Good. Warwick could learn what magic was afoot without their interruption. A quick search led him to a ladder up the back of the float. He climbed, testing the air with each step.

At the top, he felt a vibration, slippery and malevolent. A careful observation showed a black haze swirling around the perimeter of the float, not unlike the mist which dwelled within the detective.

Perhaps this was the true draw. Like magic to like magic. Mlle. Georgette's report of the boy who was stolen from her might just be a coincidence. While the black magic beckoned to the unknowing detective.

Interesting.

It might mean the dark magic within Thibodeaux had more of a hold on him than Warwick thought. Or . . . Warwick strained to see further. Held his hand close without touching the nearly invisible barrier. He sniffed the air.

"Barathrum!" Warwick cursed. "What a sapskull am I?"

At this, Thibodeaux looked around the end of the statue.

"I fear I have found the stolen boy, detective."

Chapter 24

SABINE

Sabine's eyes still burned. It must be from the late afternoon light cutting through the window. Surely they couldn't still be irritated from her disreputable cry a half hour ago. But who knew about such things?

Sabine hadn't had a friend whose shoulder she could cry on. Or who wanted to cry on hers, even if she was nearly a foot shorter. So maybe Meg had mostly been crying in Sabine's hair rather than on her shoulder. Didn't matter, it was still a new and slightly disturbing experience for Sabine.

Neither of them spoke as they searched through the tidy, if outrageously colorful, kitchen. The only sound was the opening and closing of cabinets and drawers, and banging and clattering of pots and pans. Sabine had not been brave enough to try the refrigerator. Afraid that the food from last fall was still there, forming its own colony. Perhaps establishing an uprising. Who knew? If she opened the door, an army of anarchist mold samples might attack.

"If it were really bad," Meg said, guessing at the cause of Sabine's scowl. "The whole room would smell. Whoever cleaned this place up probably cleaned the fridge out, too."

"I'm not sure that the guys in HAZMAT suits who clean up blood and bodies are the Merry Maids type," Sabine said. She stared at the refrigerator from across the room, ready to duck under the table if Meg was attacked. Mighty brave of me, she thought. Still, she was ready to duck.

The latch creaked from little use. The refrigerator door stuck and Meg gave it a tug. It swung open, hit the cabinet, and bounced back. Surprisingly, no invading spore army erupted into the kitchen. That was positive. Meg opened it wider. Inside, the shelves looked as clean as the windows. Only a box of baking soda, several bottles of water, and a few canned sodas sat on the shelves.

"Feel lucky?" Meg asked as she reached for the freezer.

"Go for it."

Nothing jumped out. Instead, inside was an assortment of frozen foods.

"So," Sabine raised her eyebrows. "We obviously have a case of house elves."

"Aren't those called brownies?" Meg asked.

"Who's the expert on magic here?" Sabine said testily.

Meg grunted in reply.

Sabine walked over to observe the contents. Not bad. Zatarain's Red Beans & Rice frozen dinners. Pepperoni and veggie pizzas. Frozen okra and butter beans. And a tub of mint chocolate chip ice cream. Well, you can't win them all. She examined the carton, not opened.

"Nothing's been opened," Meg said.

"The brownies shop as well as clean. Interesting."

Sabine's satchel buzzed in response.

"What did you steal that buzzes? A swarm of cicadas? A testy alarm clock?"

"I prefer the term liberated," Sabine said.

"Call it what you like. Let's see what you've got."

Sabine pulled the strap over her head, taking the comfortable weight off her shoulder. She set the satchel on the kitchen table with Meg hovering over her.

"Give me a little space," Sabine said. "Remember those swarming wasps I told you about?"

"I'd rather they were cicadas," Meg said, but took a step back.

Sabine wasn't used to all this friendly huggy friend stuff. It wasn't terrible. She just wasn't sure what to do with it yet. Ignoring that thought for the time being, she unbuckled and lifted the flap of the satchel. Jewel tones glowed from the interior, causing her eyes to water again. At least this time, she was sure it was the light and not those pesky feelings.

"You stole glow sticks? What, for the parade?"

"They don't use glow sticks at the Mardi Gras parade."

"I've never been before. How was I supposed to know?" Meg said a little testily.

Good. Sabine was more comfortable with this type of interaction.

"Has the parade even happened yet?"

"It's tonight."

"It seemed like it was months away."

"It *was* months away. Now, it's tonight."

They were both quiet for a moment. Sabine felt guilt settle on her shoulders. While she thought Meg was off gallivanting for a few days longer than normal, she'd been on the other side for months. From the seeping wounds on her arm, it hadn't been a good few months. Meg took a hitch breath, and Sabine feared the blame that was about to be heaped on top of her. She hunched her shoulders, readying for the below.

Meg sniffled. "You were going to come after me."

Worried that this was about to turn into another weeping session, Sabine jumped in to change the subject. "Back to the glow sticks."

Meg rubbed the back of her hand across her nose and inched up beside Sabine. They leaned over the satchel, blinking against the bright light, when something large and black and covered in feathers crashed into the window.

Sabine yelped, jumped, and knocked her bag over. Its contents tumbled out across the plastic tablecloth. "Great. Now, we're being attacked by buzzards."

Black wings beat against the glass. Not a buzzard, a crow. A big one. But Sabine wasn't amending her statement until she'd checked it out. She shoved the window open along swollen wooden tracks. The bird wedged its way inside. It hopped off the sill and into the sink, where it fluffed its feathers, spraying water across the counter.

"Still wet from last night's rain?" Sabine asked, more gently than she'd meant to. A treacherous part of her hoped she knew this particular fowl feathered friend. It would seem she was getting accustomed to this whole friend business quicker than she liked.

"At least it's courteous enough to do that in the sink," Meg said.

"What are you doing here?" Sabine barked at the bird.

"Isn't that your friend?" Meg approached it warily, as one should approach an unknown creepy crow.

"I don't have any crow friends." Sabine had snapped out the words a little too quickly. They rang false even to her own ears.

She stalked up to the bird and bent over, putting them eye to eye.

"If he's not your friend, you might not want to put your eyeballs so close to his beak," Meg pointed out.

The crow twisted its head, eyeing the two of them suspiciously.

"Well?" Sabine demanded, her pulse racing with a hope she'd deny if asked.

Creeek. And it made sense! Well, as much as a smack talking crow friend of a witch ever makes sense.

Relief flooded her, but Sabine tamped it down hard and crossed her arms. "Oh, so now you come back, banging against my window, hoping to get in. I should have left you and your pestilent plumage outside. You know what I went through all by myself last fall?"

"That's not how I remembered hearing the story," Meg said.

Crooooaaak, the crow croaked.

Sabine narrowed her eyes.

The crow hopped onto the counter and paced the length, muttering, *Wonk-wonk.* It flapped its wings. *Toc-ca, Toc-cak,* it finished with a hoarse rattling from deep in the back of its throat.

"Fine," Sabine said, relaxing her arms. "If you say so. It's just I'm missss—" She hissed herself to a stop, just short of admitting to missing the foul fowl.

"What did it say?" Meg followed the crow down the counter, mesmerized. It stopped, and she gently stroked the feathers between its wings. The crow bowed its head, allowing her to caress the end of his beak.

"Oh, yeah. You don't speak crow."

"Yeah."

Sabine shrugged. "He says he's been feasting from dumpsters, pooping on statues, and generally partaking in all the pestilent plumage activities."

Craaank! The bird jabbed at Sabine, who was just out of reach. She didn't bother flinching, and instead, cocked an eyebrow at the bird, daring it to contradict her.

It ignored her while Meg gave her the stink-eye.

"Fine," Sabine relented. "He's been in the Beyond. He went to find Valdi's killer, only to find out she hadn't been killed at all. You'd have known that if you'd stayed here," she told the bird.

Meg flinched at that, and Sabine felt a pang of regret for letting her mouth get the better of her.

"Anyway, he got trapped. Had to trade his voice to get out. That's why I couldn't understand him before."

"But you do now."

"Yeah. What's up with that?" Sabine asked the crow.

Crocka, it began and continued clicking and rattling until it was done.

Sabine stroked the bottom of its neck, lifting a silver ring that had lain hidden under his feathers. Seed pearls in light purple, dark pink, and blue hung from the bottom.

"This," she tapped the pearls, "allows his—"

Cranky.

"I am not your familiar. You mangy feather duster."

Crrooaaa.

"Whatever." Sabine backed away.

Meg continued petting it.

Crocka, cr-r-r-uck.

Sabine snorted.

"Translation, please." Meg cooed at the pest.

"He says his name is not actually Pestilent Plumage. It's Bertrand."

"Really?"

Creeeek, the crow creaked.

"He says Bertrand is an old French name, meaning 'crow.' Originating from the Germanic word for—"

Craaw, Craaw!

"Oh, give me a break." Sabine rolled her eyes so hard they ached. "The Germanic word for 'magnificent crow.' A bit pompous, don't you think?"

Bertrand ruffled his feathers.

Intervening in the rising storm, Meg lifted the pearls one at a time from under Bertrand's ruff. "Berty, what an adorable name."

The crow spread his wings and bobbed his head at her.

"Get a room, you two." Sabine turned her back on the two lovebirds. In front of her, the table was strewn with credit cards, dollar bills, and brilliant orbs of light. Like gems encrusting the flowered plastic tablecloth.

Creeek. The jewels had caught Bertrand's attention, too.

Only they weren't really jewels. They didn't seem to have physical form.

"Oooh," Meg reached for an Emerald Green pulsing light. Her fingers brushed the rays, and she snatched her hand back. "Ouch!"

"Those were in your bag and they didn't zap you?" she said accusingly.

"I'm a witch."

"Barely," Meg mumbled.

Sabine reached for a deep, pulsing purple.

Craaw, Craaw!

She snatched her hand back before touching the radiating light.

"Fine. What are they?"

Cr-r-u-uck.

Sabine's eyes flew wide open.

"Was that as bad as it sounded?" Meg asked.

"Worse."

Caw!

Chapter 25

THIBODEAUX

Jean-Luc's stomach roiled at the thought of that black smoke filling the apartment where he'd been trapped last fall. It'd come with him, stayed with him, grew inside him. Going up the ladder of the Eros Mardi Gras float took an act of courage that he wasn't sure he had. But if the goblin was right, someone was trapped up there, someone who needed his help, and that was what Detective Thibodeaux did. It was his job. It was who he was.

"So, I just walk into it?" he asked the gnarled man.

"It shouldn't stop you from entering." The goblin debated his next words. "I cannot go in with you. The dark magic . . . it would take me if I did."

"All right. You stay here and stay out of sight."

"It should let you out, unless it was set to take you as well."

That brought Thibodeaux to a stop, his hands on the rungs of the latter and one foot halfway up. He stepped back. "How do we find out if it is or not?"

"We don't."

It's your job. Get up there, he told himself. He felt a familiar electrical zap as he stepped onto the float, and green light arced around him like lightning.

"Be careful up there," called the artist from down below. She hadn't wanted to let the detective on the float, but he'd given her a 'you realize I'm the police' look. He didn't like to throw it around too often, but if someone was trapped up there the way he'd been trapped, he had to help. She agreed to let him up, but followed his progress around the end of the float and down the sides, keeping a sharp eye on his movements, suspecting even an officer might be out to vandalize her hard work.

The Bacchus parade was that night. She was cutting it close, finishing the repairs. Some krewes were already sculpting figures for next year. She didn't have time to make additional repairs, she told him, rather tersely.

Passing by a well-muscled calf, Jean-Luc looked up the side of what must be a depiction of the god Eros. The top of Jean-Luc's head reached the statue's waist. As he approached, he came face-to-bum with a rounded butt cheek peeking out from under a sculpted toga.

"I thought he was supposed to be a baby," he called down to the woman who was still giving him the eye. "You know, little with round cheeks and wings and a diaper."

"That's Cupid, the Roman version. Eros is Greek," she yelled up with a disdainful look, painfully similar to one a petite thief he knew often wore.

Feeling rather like a perv, he checked beneath the statue's legs for any opening or shackles or hidden person. Truth be told, he had no idea what he was looking for. He'd expected to walk through a wall of smoke like that which had shot out of the French market, like the one that had encased him in the apartment last fall, like the black tendrils that swam behind his eyes.

Yet he saw nothing of the sort.

Jean-Luc walked the length of the float, past sculptures of adoring women and fawning men draped across one another in the throes of passion. All tastefully, if obscurely, covered with robes. Rosie flushes stained their cheeks, lips parted as if they had just exhaled. Jean-Luc felt himself flush, as if he were walking through the middle of a fantasy orgy of some kind.

Circling twice, he came to a stop again in front of the God statue. There were no hidden spaces that he could find. He'd even knocked on a few statues to see if they were hollow, which earned him a bark from the woman below.

He was grateful that no human seemed to notice the goblin. It saved Jean-Luc a lot of time explaining. But right about now, it would be nice if attention were turned to Warwick and off of him. One more time around, as he passed the last sculpted couple huddled together behind the god's legs, he was convinced no one was trapped up here.

The scarred skin across his calf howled in pain, tripping him to a stop. He braced himself on the god's thigh to catch his breath. The ill healed wound pulsed. He breathed through pursed lips in an attempt to get the pain under control when a black smudge crossed his vision.

Jean-Luc closed his eyes, counted to three, and opened them again. He turned his head left and right, hoping that it was a trick of the shadows. Whether his eyes were open or closed, it was still there.

Black mist swirled and grew, blotting out his vision of the brightly lit warehouse. He could no longer see the god or the sculpted couple. Nothing but grasping, undulating blackness.

He could tell it was hungry. And he felt himself respond, growing predatory.

His eyesight cleared enough to make out the shapes around him. The glossy paint of Eros's toga, the pink of an amour's cheeks, and the gleam in an eye were all dulled. Yet, he could make out the forms in muted color.

Cowering under the great Eros, clinging to his well-sculpted leg, a man in his early twenties looked up at Jean-Luc. He wore a goatee muted by days' worth of stubble. The whites of his eyes were mapped with red lines, and the skin underneath was bruised. Jean-Luc had seen that expression on his own face once.

"Can you see me?" Jean-Luc asked.

The young man's eyes remained unfocused, roaming from Jean-Luc's shoes to the surrounding statues and up through the mists, swirling around the hazed lights. They crossed over Jean-Luc's face and ventured off before realization hit, and they darted back. The man's mouth opened as if asking a question. His eyes pleaded as he reached up for Jean-Luc, who held out a hand to help him up, but one passed through the other.

This was the face Jean-Luc had found from a search of the Eros's Krewe website. This was the face described to him by Georgette, the shop owner. And it was eerily similar to the face of the heartless man found on the Canal Streetcar. And the missing Tyler Davis from last fall.

Whomever trapped this man seemed to have a preferred type. But how did that fit with the man on the streetcar? Or was Jean-Luc trying to make too many connections that might all be a matter of coincidence?

This man, Oliver, let go of Eros and grabbed for Jean-Luc's leg. The detective felt the track of the panicked man's hand as it passed over and through his pulsing wound without catching hold. Oliver fell and face planted on the boards of the float. He grappled for purchase on the detective's pants leg.

Jean-Luc could not help but remember how he had grasped for Sabine when she'd come looking for him in Davis's apartment months ago. How she had heard something, sensed something, but could not see him or hear him.

He stepped back, and the man crawled after him. The mists clouded over his vision so that he could barely see the desperate man through the darkness. But Jean-Luc refused to leave him alone. He crouched, his wounded leg screaming, and reached into the darkness, feeling the man's hand close finally on his.

Standing to haul the man out with him, a call from below broke his focus, and Jean-Luc lost his grip. The mists cleared, leaving only air between the god sculpture's legs.

"NO!" Jean-Luc roared in outrage.

"Hey!" the artist yelled. "What're you doing up there?"

The mists billowed, obscuring Oliver, hand out, screaming, and was gone again.

Jean-Luc cursed the woman and the god. The shadow of the giant sculpture cast across the reclining couple. Their cheeks were again rosy. Their seeking mouths and eyes bright. He shoved the sculpted the couple aside, and clawed at the god's legs, leaving gouges in its painted surface.

The air remained clear of mists. The man gone. Beyond his help.

"Where did he go?" Jean-Luc demanded of the goblin. Warwick cut his eyes to the woman and gave a minute shake of his head.

"I told you Oliver wasn't here," the woman said. "Now, get off the float. I don't care if you are the police." The artist had started up the ladder after him until Jean-Luc threw out a hand. She jolted to a stop, a look of fear followed by uncertainty, then anger crossed in quick succession across her face.

Her knuckles went white as she gripped the ladder, not backing down. Her gaze landed on the gouges in the statue. Her eyes were flint and her voice sparked. "You heard me. Down."

A shudder of revulsion at his complete ineptness wracked Jean-Luc's frame. He forced a nod and approached the ladder slowly to show he was not dangerous. Though he could feel violence roiling within him.

Chapter 26

MEGAN

Y ou. Stole. What?" Meg enunciated each word separately. "Do you even know how to use them?"

"Sure."

"Show me."

"I'm not sure which is which yet."

More squawks from the crow.

Meg fancied that she might be able to understand it, almost. Or maybe she just understood the sentiment of amazement and appall that Sabine was willing and capable of screwing up this big.

"You stole Mlle. Georgette's magic without knowing what to do with it?"

"I'll figure it out," Sabine shrugged, as if it was no big deal. When it was *absolutely* a big deal to steal spells from a witch. Or Meg assumed it would be. Assuming she was a real witch. Sabine seemed to be, if only just barely. So, why not the owner of the Sassy Witch, too?

Sabine held her satchel open under the edge of the table, raked the glowing loot back in, and secured the flap. "I didn't exactly know that I was stealing it at the time."

"What do you *think* they do?"

Sabine peeked in the bag. "One must be for levitation. I must've used it when she threw me off the balcony to stop myself from hitting the pavement. But maybe I used it up and don't have it anymore."

They both looked to the crow for confirmation. It ticked at them and turned its back. Not very helpful. These creatures and their magic were proving much less magical than she would've imagined as a child.

"I'll deal with the spells. You pull out that bracelet and start remembering stuff."

"Changing the subject does not mean you don't have a satchel full of bombs."

"Probably not bombs."

"You said she threw fireballs."

"I said I was *pretty sure* she did. I didn't stop to check. Now, tell me what the charms have to say."

Meg pulled out the bracelet from her purse, pinching it between two fingers. "You never answered me. How'd she get it?"

"Start remembering. Then maybe you can tell me." Sabine cocked her head, then grabbed for the bracelet, but Meg held it out of her reach. "That one," she pointed. "The heart charm. Try it. That was on the necklace Georgette wore when I first met her."

Meg shook the bracelet and watched it sway, the charms clattering softly against one another. Her mouth tightened and her shoulders tensed.

"Go ahead. Start." Sabine prodded.

"I don't think I want to."

"Come on. It'll probably help with the heartache stuff."

"Georgette has nothing to do with it." Meg scowled.

"You don't know that. You have her heart charm."

"The charm has nothing to do with me and . . . and . . ."

"Fair enough. Then this will be the perfect distraction, *because* it has nothing to do with you and Valdi. So find out what it is Georgette is hiding. And why she has a charm on your bracelet."

"Maybe we should do it later." Meg tucked it back in her pocket, but kept her fingers curled around it.

"We need to know what those creatures are doing that sends you back here in tatters."

Meg felt a heat rising up her neck and over her cheeks, a mix of humiliation and anger. She had to regain some control over her life. "Do you agree to us living here, if I do?"

"Sure. Even though we have no clue what kind of creature has been cleaning up the place."

Meg cocked an eyebrow at her. "I think we know. Who's the one person with access to a key, who knew about the murder, and who would also do anything to help you?"

"No one."

Croacka.

Meg stroked Bertrand's glossy feathers. "You're right, Bertie. She's just too stubborn to admit it."

"You don't know what he said," Sabine accused.

"Close enough. Do you want me to tell you what we think?"

"No."

"Fine." Meg pulled the bracelet back out. "Maybe I should sit down before retrieving the memories." She headed to the living room.

"You're stalling." Sabine followed on her heals. "Just do it and I'll . . . I'll let you eat all the chocolate mint ice cream by yourself." There had to be a catch somewhere. But with Sabine, she'd likely never figure it out.

Sitting on the garish yet cozy couch, Meg fluffed the pillows and pulled up the Ottoman.

"Stalling."

Crucka.

With a glare at the two of them, Meg pinched the heart charm between her fingers.

A chilled breeze blew across her face. The smell of rotten ice and desire met her nose. She looked past the hazy living room walls and out a pointed stone arch at a frozen landscape. Skeletal trees were coated with ice. Heavy clouds hung over miles and miles of frozen land with a crystal lake in the distance.

Reflections in the window caught two figures behind her. One, a woman in snug fitting pants and bodice, dark and foreboding, a storm cloud forming over her expression. The other tall and icy. His expression sharp and lovely. Meg's breath caught.

"What is it? What did you see?" Sabine's voice came muffled to Meg's ears, startling her.

Feeling the cushy couch under her once more, she focused on Sabine. "Keep quiet. I can't do it with you hovering."

"Wait before you do it again. Tell me what you saw."

"Georgette."

"Oh, yeah. I knew that charm belonged to her. Anyone else? It sounded like people were talking."

"You heard it?" Meg squirmed on the cushions. She wasn't sure if she wanted anyone else to have a firsthand view of what had happened until she saw it for herself.

"I heard mumbles. No words. Who was it?"

"A tall, cold man." It was a stupid description, so Meg added, "I think I've seen him before."

"Yeah, I'd say you have. Pale white hair, sharp teeth, icy blue eyes, and a blue tinged to his skin. Kinda hot but scary looking?"

"That's him. I couldn't see his eyes, but I know they were blue, somehow." It unnerved Meg that Sabine remembered bits of her past better than she did. "Do you think it's the same Fae from before?

"I'd bet anything it is." Instead of smug, Sabine looked angry. Her jaw was clenched, and she fisted her hands. If cartoon puffs of smoke came from her ears, Meg wouldn't have been surprised.

"Great." Having Sabine mad on her behalf gave Meg validation. No damned Fae got to use her and steal her memories of the act. Not anymore. "Alright, I'm going back in."

In the chilled room, Meg studied the two figures in the reflection.

The witch, Georgette, cut her eyes to Meg's back. "Why is my salesclerk here? You need a new set of tarot cards?"

"Megan Armand and I are old acquaintances," the icy man replied with a cool air.

Georgette's expression turned sour. "She has no heart to give you. A cold woman."

"So Megan says. But everyone has a heart."

"Not if they've given it away," Georgette said, her tone sharp and sullen.

The Meg in Sabine's aunt's living room gasped.

The Meg in the icy room did not.

"What? What?" Sabine asked repeatedly.

In the living room Meg waved her off. She didn't know if the witch knew she'd given her heart away, but Meg planned on finding out what was going on.

Inside the icy room, Meg asked, "Why are you here, Georgette?"

"You see this?" Georgette unhooked her corset and spread it open wide. Behind it, ribs protruded like broken teeth, glistening around a gaping hole in the witch's chest. Inside the cavity rested a shriveled heart, struggling to beat.

"This will be you soon," Georgette told her. "He'll ask for your heart and you will rip it out of your own chest and give it to him."

Meg's gaze drifted back to the lump of heart in Georgette's chest.

Georgette hid it with a hand possessively. "Once he's taken yours, you'll search for another. Take someone else's, but it will not be enough."

Behind her, the Fae smirked, pleased at the spectacle.

To Meg's horror, Georgette took the rotten, beating heart from her chest and threw it on the floor at Meg's feet. "There, you can have that one. I am done with it and will soon have another."

The Fae tutted behind her. "Only if he gives it freely, my pet. You know the rules. Last time you grew too eager. And look at the result."

They both stared at the pitiful heart on the cold tiles. It beat slower and slower, then stopped. Horrified by the act and sorrowful for whomever the heart had belonged to, Meg stooped to pick it up.

Georgette shoved her aside to snatch up the dead thing and clasped it to her bosom.

Meg scrambled away and shoved to her feet. "Who's heart is that?"

Georgette stroked the slick organ protectively, and the Fae answered for her. "It belonged to Georgette's last conquest. She did not find the first in time, did you, my pet?" he said to the witch. "Now, it would seem that Georgette has lured the boy of your desires to her bed in hopes of taking his."

Meg searched through her memory for any man that she and Georgette both knew. The cold-hearted Fae watching them like they were dogs in a fight was the only male they had in common. Then Meg's mind landed upon another possible option.

"Oliver?"

Georgette's answering sneer told her she was correct.

Meg averted her eyes from the intensity in the woman's eyes.

"Is my pet, Megan, jealous of Georgette?" The sparkle in the Fae's eye said he hoped it was true.

Meg straightened herself. She had to leave. She had to warn Oliver about these two. But she sensed she needed to placate the two of them if she hoped to leave intact.

"Oliver is welcome to give his heart to whomever he wants." Meg just hoped that wasn't as literal.

"He will." Georgette practically sparked with spite.

The Fae smiled his sharp smile. Baylur, that was his name. Meg could almost remember calling his name, and him coming to her. She shied away from the other memories of him that arose.

Georgette turned her back to the Fae and spoke low for Meg's ears only. "You will give up your hardened heart. We all do in the end." She almost sounded wistful before turning to the Fae. "I'm leaving. We'll see who wins this round, you or I. Megan is weak, but she still fights you. And Oliver is mine already."

As the witch left the room, Baylur stalked toward Meg, his hand out, palm up. He wore an expression of adoration, but it was only a mask. His cruel eyes shone through.

She should have felt fear, but she only felt empty.

Chapter 27

WARWICK

The aged wooden boards of the old river walk were dark and grooved, weathered by years of storms from the Gulf. Thibodeaux's steps thudded back and forth.

"How do I draw it out, the black smoke? When it rises, I can see him. It's the missing man the witch described."

Warwick could feel the dark magic seething underneath the detective's skin. "Let it stay buried," he whispered to the air and to the worn boards and to the river that ran to the sea. "Let him win out over it."

Thibodeaux spun around and stomped back the way he'd come. His brow tight. His mouth a scowl. His hands flexing, ready for a fight. Warwick could see him trying and failing to reach into the well of blackness deep within. He'd suppressed it. Now it would not come to his call. Not yet.

Given time, it would.

Thibodeaux cursed as he came to a halt just short of running into the goblin. Warwick barely reached the man's chest. He blended into the old wood, invisible to onlookers. Unless a person looked directly at him, he disappeared.

"Bring it back!" the detective demanded.

Warwick met the man's crazed eyes. "You do not want to call it to the surface. Let it sleep until you can purge it from your system."

He dared to clutch Warwick's shoulders, his hands tightening against the century old being, and stopped himself short of shaking him. "Oliver's on that float. I saw him calling for help. I had his hand in mine."

Warwick stepped back and brushed the detective's hands from his jacket. He would forgive the human this transgression. This hulking, earnest man, who fought to do right against forces he could not understand, had won some begrudging respect from Warwick, a goblin of the Great Goblin Court of King Philip I.

"I could see him and touch him. Then he was gone." Thibodeaux ran a hand through his hair and resumed pacing. "If the painter hadn't called my name. If my concentration hadn't broken. I could have done it. I could have saved him."

His face was flush as if with fever or anger. Warwick did not have a full grasp of these beings and their fluid emotions.

"He had a watch. I saw it. Hanging on a chain around his neck. If it counts down, it could be the end. It could stop his heart like it tried to stop mine."

Warwick stepped in front of him. The detective jolted. From his perspective, Warwick would have simply appeared where he was not before. A deep V creased the man's brow.

"The timepiece was not meant for you," Warwick warned him.

"This one, the one around his neck. It's set for him, isn't it? You gave it to whoever trapped that boy."

Ah, this was anger.

"He is a man, not a boy. He made choices which earned him the timepiece." Warwick reasoned away the irrational twinge of guilt tormented him.

"You know how it works and what it does. You have to stop it."

"I cannot."

Simple humans and their rudimentary knowledge of the market and its laws.

"Then what use are you?" Thibodeaux bellowed, and a flock of seagulls shrieked in protest as they launched from the metal roof of the warehouse holding the floats. They had no tolerance for this human's tantrums. And Warwick's ran thin as well.

He did not answer, giving the human time to reflect and offer his apology.

He did not.

Warwick let himself fade from view, merging with the boards beneath him.

Thibodeaux roared in frustration, and darkness flickered in his eyes.

The reverberation of the dark magic rising in the detective shattered Warwick's glamour. He saw the man startle at his appearance, but he quickly faded again. He would not aid the man with the darkness so close to the surface.

Thibodeaux cursed and paced and cursed some more.

"I'll call the parade to a halt until I can get him out. Or at the least, have the float pulled from the lineup. The clock is probably set to count down in the middle of the parade. Create a big scene with a dead body. Why else trap him on the float? We stop the float; it ruins the killer's plan." Nodding to himself, convinced of his own conclusion.

"Come on," Thibodeaux impudently called to Warwick. "We have to go to headquarters."

The detective headed for his car and reached the parking lot before realizing Warwick did not follow.

"Are you coming?"

"What will you tell them?" Warwick tried reasoning with the simple creature. Though they stood apart, he let his voice carry between them without raising it. "They do not know of us. They cannot understand. They will not listen."

There, those were simple enough terms for a simple mind. Though Warwick suspected this one might be brighter than most.

"That's why you have to come. When they see you, what you are, they'll believe." Thibodeaux beckoned for Warwick to hurry.

Ah, not as bright as Warwick had hoped. He was so seldom wrong. Yet it could be the dark magic within clouding the man's thoughts.

Yes, Warwick had not been incorrect in his assessment. He would remain and help in what way he could for Thibodeaux's sake, but he would not allow the sort of display the man suggested.

"I am not an exhibit. Even if I were to allow it. They would see what they chose to see in exclusion of reality. You are unique, Detective Jean-Luc Thibodeaux." Warwick did not part with such praise easily.

This did not mollify the man.

Frustrated and furious, Thibodeaux stalked back toward the river and Warwick. His eyes held the crazed expression of one obsessed. This would not do.

Warwick faded into the background.

The detective blinked and turned his head, as if to catch Warwick in his peripheral vision. He *was* a smart one. Maybe he *could* win against the darkness within.

Warwick wished him well, but kept his glamour in place.

Chapter 28

SABINE

Meg fell away from the memory of the Ice Palace, clutching at her chest in the dim living room. Sabine hovered over her. Bertrand perched on the back of the couch, peering over her shoulder, muttering nervously, and flaring his wings.

"I think they're going to kill Oliver," Meg gasped.

"Who?" Sabine asked.

"Georgette. Baylur. I don't know." Meg's eyes cleared from the haze of reading the charm. She popped up off the couch, knocking Sabine back. "They are going to rip his heart out. Or he's going to rip it out and give it to them."

"Who's Baylur?"

"The Fae. Tall, icy, terrifying."

"Oh," Sabine said. "The Iceman."

Craaw, Craaw!

"We have to find him. We have to warn him. But I don't know where he lives."

Sabine stepped out of her way as Meg stalked past, still half lost in the memory. "Do you know where he lives?"

"No. But it's early enough. He'll be at the Sassy Witch." Meg made for the door, but Sabine stopped her.

"Georgette said he's not coming back there. And it sounded pretty permanent. Like scary permanent."

"Fine. Fine. But we have to tell him."

"He wouldn't actually rip out his heart and hand it to them, would he?" Sabine couldn't fathom such a thing.

Meg rounded on her. "You know how Georgette's corset always looked kind of icky and damp?" Sabine nodded. "She showed me why."

"I'm not sure I want to know."

"You don't," Meg said, then proceeded to tell her in detail what she had seen in the memory from the gaping hole in the witch's chest to the rotting heart inside.

Sabine doubled over, dry heaving, but succeeded in holding the contents of her stomach down the best she could. Not wanting to mess up the pre-cleaned house again. She held a hand up until she could get control of stomach, then said, "Okay, where do we start looking for him?"

Cracka-Cracka.

Meg snapped her fingers and pointed at the crow. "You're right."

Sabine didn't know what to make of that interaction.

"Oliver invited me to work with him down at the warehouse where they build the floats for the Mardi Gras parade. He's in a krewe. He'll be there. You said it was tonight, right?"

"We'll never be able to find them in all the chaos," Sabine said.

"We have to try. Come on. I'll drive." Meg dug in her pocket for the keys and stormed out the door.

"Of course you will. I don't have a car."

Croooaaak.

"Shut up."

Winding their way through traffic was excruciating. One road after another was blocked off in preparation for the parade. Meg threw her phone at Sabine and talked her through the mechanics of pulling up a map app and finding a route to a specific warehouse on the banks of the river.

They had to park several blocks away. Meg jumped from the car and took off at a jog, pointing her keys over her shoulder to lock the doors. With a much shorter gait, Sabine had to sprint to keep up.

Bertrand streaked ahead of them, just above the crowd, for them to follow. Sabine assumed it was him because he kept up a running chatter along the way. She couldn't understand what he said from that distance, but surely no other crow was that mouthy.

People congregated outside the doors to the warehouse. Many already half drunk. The rest, fully drunk. Most wearing costumes. A few masks.

"How are we going to find pretty boy behind a mask?" Sabine asked between panted breaths. Bertrand circled overhead, landed on Sabine's shoulder long enough to squawk in her ear, then soared over the crowds and into the warehouse.

"Bertrand is going to look for him," Sabine translated for Meg. "He doesn't seem to think Oliver is out here. Let's see if we can shove our way inside."

Meg grabbed Sabine's arm and plowed a path through. Sabine had never seen her so assertive. Once inside, she peeled

Meg's hand from around her arm as the tall woman barked instructions at her.

"You circle left. I'll circle right. We meet up at the Eros float." Meg started to take off, but Sabine stopped her.

"What is an Eros float?"

"The Greek god."

Sabine opened her eyes wide to show how useless that information was in a warehouse full of floats dedicated to Greek gods.

Meg shook her head in frustration. "God of love and fornication."

"Got it, Cupid. Cute baby little wings and a diaper."

Meg grabbed Sabine by the shoulders and pulled her close. "Not the Roman god. The Greek one. Young, male, totally sexy, surrounded by lovers."

"Like the Fae."

"Got it. Now go." Meg shoved her in one direction and took off in the other.

"There's no way this could go wrong," Sabine grumbled.

Croooaaak.

"You got that right." Sabine wedged her way between masked figures, looking for anyone about the right height and build and sporting a haughty goatee while yelling, "Oliver!"

Chapter 29

THIBODEAUX

S pitting another lengthy string of curses, Jean-Luc sprinted for the car. He did not have time to play around. A life was at stake. He knew what it felt like to have your heart tied to a ticking clock, one that wound down to your death. Slamming a blue light onto his dash, he wove through the streets of New Orleans, a slow and grueling speed no matter how he pushed.

Jean-Luc barreled through the doors, one after the other until he reached his office at police headquarters. Officer Williams looked up and smiled when the detective came in, only to have that smile wither and die when he took in Jean-Luc's scowl. Williams stood to greet him despite the expression.

"Good to see you up and working." The cheerful man bobbed his head in agreement with himself. He had a handful of paperwork, probably still filing his report from his beat at the market.

Jean-Luc walked past with a curt nod, but Williams fell into step with him.

"After last night, I thought you might have to call in. Your leg was pretty messed up. But Carmichael said she'd heard from you, and you were investigating another missing person?" When he received no reply, Williams continued. "Have you had a chance to see the forensics report yet on the streetcar victim?"

That finally got Jean-Luc's attention. He held the door and waved Williams into the office with him before shutting it. Williams took a seat, looking eager, while Jean-Luc scanned the folder on his desk. A series of photos caught his eye.

"What's this?"

"That's the cool part." Williams looked so eager that Jean-Luc wouldn't have been surprised if the man hadn't waited for him just to see his reaction. A set of glossy photos showed what looked like two-inch-long spikes or blades. They pricked at a recent memory, but Jean-Luc couldn't hone in on it.

"They're metal fingernails," the officer filled in the picture for him.

They looked like a pewter version of the shop owner's bronzed nails from the Sassy Witch earlier that morning.

Had that all happened today?

"Were they found on the scene?"

"More like in it." Williams laughed. Seeing the detective did not get the joke, he elaborated. "The nails were extracted from the inside of the chest cavity, buried in all that charred flesh." Williams shuddered at the recollection, but the grin never left his face.

Jean-Luc would need to go back and talk to Mlle. Georgette again. He remembered the apparent glee with which she'd told him that Oliver had been 'stolen.' Could she be responsible for trapping him? Were she and her wicked nails connected to the streetcar victim?

"Start running DNA on the nails. Right now, I need to talk to Fitzgerald. It's urgent." Jean-Luc left the office, as he was about to say something else.

"I haven't seen her. She's probably in her office," Williams called after him.

"Seen who?" asked Carmichael, who stood just outside Jean-Luc's office.

"The superintendent."

"I heard you were here, and I was just coming to give you a heads up that she wants to talk with you." Carmichael's eyes scanned his face as if she were waiting for something.

"Good, I've got to get her to sequester a parade float." Jean-Luc's headlong rush to instigate the plan was stopped when Carmichael laid a hand on his biceps and squeezed. He stopped and looked at her, confused.

"Jean-Luc," she spoke in a low voice, looking over his shoulder to see if Williams was still there. Apparently, he was, but took her hint and moved on. "Fitzgerald thinks you might need to take some time off."

Carmichael paused, averting her eyes from the look Jean-Luc gave her, but didn't stop. She leaned in and spoke more intimately. He pulled back, but her grip tightened.

"I'm worried, too. You haven't been yourself. Not since . . ." she paused again, but it felt this time like it was calculated. "Not since last fall."

Jean-Luc jerked out of her grip before realizing they had an audience of officers. He straightened his jacket and they all suddenly had some other place to be. No time to spare for interoffice politics or for Carmichael's misguided attention. He wound his way through the labyrinth of corridors to Superintendent Fitzpatrick's office.

She waved him in and he shut the door behind him, harder than he'd intended. The door slammed into the frame, and the receptionist squeaked outside. Fitzpatrick merely raised an eyebrow at him and pointed to the seat across from her, but he was too wound up to sit.

"Listen, I need a float sequestered from the parade tonight."

The look on her face told him he needed to tread more carefully. Warwick's warning rang in his ears. Maybe the goblin was right, but he couldn't stand by. He was an officer. Damn it!

"Detective Thibodeaux, please take a seat. I would like to have a talk before we start pulling floats from a parade that has been planned since last year." She waited, and he relented and sat. "Thank you."

Jean-Luc jumped in before she could get started. "I have reason to believe a victim is being held on the Eros float, with plans for his murder during the parade."

That had her attention. The stern older woman leaned forward with her elbows on the desk and steepled her hands. "Can you tell me what makes you believe this?"

After opening his mouth to give her the rundown, Jean-Luc froze. How could he explain that he saw an invisible man begging for help? A man that fit the missing person's description. And was he then going to insist she arrest the witch for possibly clawing out a man's heart? Or tell her that this case was most probably related to the missing person from last fall. The one documented leaving town in a stolen car?

"Jean-Luc?"

He stared dumbly at her. Realizing his hands were knotted into fists on the arms of the chair, he relaxed them and folded them in his lap. "I . . . I think—"

The superintendent tilted her chin and looked at him over her black-rimmed glasses. "Your fellow officers have expressed concerns."

He opened his mouth to stop her, but she raised a hand and he shut it.

"And I share those concerns. I am suggesting a voluntary leave of absence—"

Jean-Luc jumped from his chair and landed with fists slamming onto her desk as he leaned into her space. "You don't understand."

He stopped at the look of surprise on her face. She recovered instantly and calmly rose on the other side of the desk, deliberately resting her fingertips on the top beside his clenched fists.

"Effective immediately. And I recommend you seek some counseling to sort out whatever it is that happened to you last fall. An incident for which you have failed to offer a full report." He tried to speak again, but she continued over him. "If I have you removed from my office, you will be put on involuntary leave following a psych evaluation."

Jean-Luc sagged back into the chair. The superintendent remained standing.

What happened? He'd had to save people. It was his job. It was who he was. And he was being sent home to 'get his head on straight,' he heard her say through the roaring in his ears.

"Thibodeaux?" She sounded concerned.

He searched his vision for the mists. This was because of them. They had tainted him and everything he did.

"Thibodeaux!"

Jean-Luc pushed up and left the office without a word.

Chapter 30

WARWICK

This edifice filled with sculptures of great creatures was at once comforting and unnerving to Warwick. It resembled vast realms of the Beyond crushed together beneath one roof. The effigies sprawled about upon their platforms, giving the appearance of life and vitality without possessing either.

The structure contained so much iron that the air itself burned Warwick's lungs. He did not know how much longer he could remain inside. But he perversely felt responsible for this witless human who found himself trapped. Perhaps it was because the honest and righteous man, Detective Jean-Luc Thibodeaux, had deemed this man worthy of saving.

Or perhaps Warwick's brain was decomposing in this toxic environment.

He allowed himself one circle of the enclosure to see what fanciful visions these people had of his kind. Some were entertaining. Many appalling. And a rare few, fairly accurate.

As he made his way back to Eros's effigy, he was surprised to spot the living representation of a satyr. It took him longer than he deemed appropriate to discern that it was merely a human on stilts in a costume. He would fault this figure for throwing his perception out of balance when he found himself in the midst of a dozen actual creatures.

Warwick had mistaken them for more humans in their remedial version of glamour. They were not.

A real satyr pranced and leapt amongst the drunken hordes without comment. Fae flowed around them. Sprites flitted about. Even goblins stood guard over effigies they found worthy.

Warwick dodged them all, weaving between wheeled carriages until he made his way back to Eros.

As he crept up to it, he was taken by surprise yet again. This time not by a creature from the Beyond, but by a human.

Megan Armand climbed atop the carriage with Eros and his sculpted devotees. This could not be good. He risked calling out to her, but before her name passed his lips, he saw another face that he recognized.

This time, Baylur did not hide himself beneath a cloak. He stood at the base of the god statue and beckoned for Meg to come to him. She had a moment of confusion upon her face. A moment in which Warwick rubbed his thumb across the moon charm in his own pocket and prayed for her wisdom.

It did him no good. He had kept the charm in his possession to give to her. To warn her from this creature. He had acted too slowly and failed her yet again.

Chapter 31

THIBODEAUX

Flashing his badge and pulling rank, Jean-Luc made it through the rows of police cars blocking off the parking lot for krewe members only. The crowd outside the warehouse slowed him down more. Once inside, he barreled his way through the crowd to the Eros float.

Warwick was nowhere to be seen. But that didn't mean he wasn't here. It just meant Jean-Luc couldn't see him. He'd hoped to find him back at Eros's float. If the goblin was there, he was carefully hidden.

Starting up the ladder, Jean-Luc was called to a halt by a slightly drunk krewe member. The man wore the requisite toga and sandals but had not yet donned his mask. Being the least inebriated in the vicinity, it must have fallen upon him to make sure no one got on the float without authorization. Jean-Luc flashed his badge, mumbled his credentials, and started back up.

"Cop or no, you can't go up there unless you're on the krewe. You should know the rules." The guy was insistent. Either his state of inebriation or his position had gone to his head if he thought he could stop Jean-Luc.

"Let's just say I *am* on the krewe," he said, continuing to climb.

The man grabbed for Jean-Luc's pant leg. "That's not gonna work."

Jean-Luc pulled back his blazer to reveal the butt of his gun in its holster. Normally, he didn't approve of such bravado. But this was not a normal circumstance. "I'm going to go up and have a look around. When I find what I've come for, I'll be back down."

That had the guy looking pretty nervous. "We ain't got nothing up there. We're not supposed to."

Ah, he was afraid Jean-Luc was looking for a drug stash. But if history proved repetitious, he'd only find coolers of liquor, which was all on the up and up for a Mardi Gras parade.

Jean-Luc decided he could afford to set the man's mind at ease. "Nothing like that. You go back to your business and hopefully, I'll be out of here before the parade starts. You keep stalling, and I'll be taking the ride with you."

The man took a step back but didn't leave. He looked around, probably trying to find someone to back him up. Not waiting for a gang of drunk, toga-clad krewe members to come attempt to drag him off, Jean-Luc stepped onto the float. The surge of electricity was stronger. Ignoring the pain, Jean-Luc made his way around the sculptures to Eros in the middle.

The black tendrils swam across his vision. He waited, but the mists didn't respond and enfold him into the space with the captive man, as he'd hoped. The costumed krewes were all filing towards their floats, paying no attention to him. Weaving to the front of the Eros Krewe was a familiar, determined woman with auburn hair pulled back tight in a ponytail.

Sabine headed his way. She must have *liberated* the toga she wore.

"Not now." Jean-Luc prayed she was just there to loot the Krewe members. But no such luck.

Climbing the ladder, she waved a mask at the self-appointed gatekeeper. When she reached the top, he handed a crate of beads up to her. Of course, she could slip onto the float with no issue.

He had to focus. Her presence would only distract him. She was just one more person he had to keep safe. But she has magic, he told himself. Not much, but more than him. As she made her way around the top of the float, he averted his eyes so that she wouldn't see the blackness rising in them.

"Thibodeaux?" She stopped on the opposite side of the sculpture of the copulating couple. "How did you know to come?"

"How did you?" he asked, uselessly, because of course she knew. Where there was trouble, there was Sabine.

Jean-Luc had to ask himself again if she was part of this. The coincidences were too large. But he didn't have time right now. Plus, he was on *voluntary* leave. He wasn't on the job. That's bullshit. And anyone that knew him would know the same. But he took the excuse.

"Have you seen Meg?" Sabine asked.

Well, he hadn't been expecting that one. "No, I'm here to get Oliver out."

"You know about them trying to rip out his heart? Meg and I came for the same reason."

Jean-Luc's blood went ice cold. "What did you say?"

Sabine narrowed her eyes. "If you don't know about the heart ripping thing, then what're you doing here?"

The blackness erupted throughout his vision. Mists consumed the whole float, yet no one noticed, including Sabine, whose eyes had blown wide and searching. He realized he must have disappeared to her.

Losing his balance, Jean-Luc reached out his hand, hitting Eros's leg. He hung on to keep from falling over. A continuous wail from within the darkness filled his ears. At Eros's feet, Oliver lay sprawled across the platform of the float, clutching at his chest. His eyes were bugged out and bloodshot. His mouth was wide open in a silent scream.

The wails came from beside him, where a woman knelt, pulling Oliver's head into her lap.

"Megan?" Jean-Luc asked.

Megan looked up. Her face tear streaked. Her eyes widened as she realized that he could see her. "Thibodeaux! Help him. It's his heart."

Jean-Luc's chest ached at the sight. He clutched his own chest in remembrance of that pain. The timepiece still hung from a necklace resting on the young man's chest.

Jean-Luc knelt and threaded his hands under Oliver's arms and pulled him to his feet. He stumbled backwards, dragging the young man. As he stepped onto the ladder, Oliver was blown back, screaming. Something would not let him pass. He reached for the wounded man, but Oliver shoved his hand aside.

Oliver lifted the clock that hung on a chain around his neck, checking the time. It was just like last fall. Jean-Luc had not been able to get out until the clock ran down.

Luckily, Meg didn't seem to have a watch or clock. He motioned for her to come to the ladder. "Let's get you out, then

I'll help Oliver. It's the clock keeping him. You don't have one, right?"

She shook her head.

"Good," Jean-Luc said on an exhale. "Quick. Sabine's here. You take her and go. I'll come back for him."

Meg hesitated but took Jean-Luc's hand when he offered it.

He stepped back onto the ladder. But when her hand touched the charmed perimeter. She snatched it back, screaming in pain.

The mists in his eyes cleared as Sabine stomped up to the edge and glared down at him as he clung to the ladder.

"What the hell was that? Your eyes went black and then you disappeared over there," she pointed behind her. "And end up over here."

Jean-Luc wrenched the rails of the ladder in frustration. "Oliver is hidden by that black smoke I told you about, and I can't get them out."

Sabine backed away from him to the center of the float, looking away. He feared she saw the blackness inside him and was revolted. However, her expression wasn't disgust, it was puzzled. The look she got when she didn't know what was going on, but was determined to find out.

"Are you sure it's the smoke stuff that's holding him?"

"I don't know." Jean-Luc took a deep breath. "But it has Meg, too."

Sabine rushed back to the ladder. "Meg is trapped in there? They'll snatch her heart, too. Go get them out of there!"

Rage rushed through him like a blazing fire. The inner blackness rose again, nearly choking him. Jean-Luc stepped up a rung until his nose just touched hers and spoke through gritted teeth. "You don't think I tried? My question is, did you come here to help or just bark at me like a yap dog?"

Her head snapped back as if she'd been struck.

They seethed at one another.

Jean-Luc contemplated wringing her neck. Literally. As the blackness blotted out his vision, he felt the pressure of violence rising in him. Instead of reaching for her, he reached around her and took hold of the mists. Without thinking whether he could or not. He jerked, and they pulled back.

"Sabine!" Meg called out. She cradled one hand to her chest. While pulling Oliver's head back into her lap. He had passed out, and his head lolled to the side, sliding out of her grip.

Sabine yelped in surprise and dove forward, but the mists tugged loose and the two wretched figures disappeared. Leaving Sabine to fall against the great god leg of Eros, howling in frustration.

An ugly part of Jean-Luc was pleased to see it. Then the mists leeched away, leaving him gutted. Think. Climbing back onto the float, he started to puzzle it out. "If I can pull back the mists. Can you pull them out?"

"If that's what's holding them and not just hiding him." Sabine motioned around the railing of the float. "There's a charm around the whole thing."

"Let's try." Jean-Luc reached for it, but it slipped through his fingers. He clamped them shut, but the mists would not answer to him this time.

Sabine watched, hope and anger and fear racing across her face.

A deep-throated laugh froze the air around the two of them. Frost formed on Sabine's lashes and ice crusted Jean-Luc's skin.

Shrieking cackles followed. An incorporeal murder of crows fluttered around them. Brushing their faces with shadow wings and scraping their skin with shadow talons.

A tall, icy man with unnaturally angular features circled one side of the god statue. The tightly corseted Georgette circled around the other side. The male spoke in a voice that made Jean-Luc's hair stand on end.

"Looks like we have two more hearts to add to our collection. A good thing, since at least one of them won't make it through the night."

Georgette ran her eyes over Jean-Luc appraisingly. "He is a bit old for my taste. But I suppose a toughened heart is better than none."

"I wouldn't mind adding another witch to my collection," the male said. He hungrily looked Sabine up and down. "And a powerful one."

Georgette snarled. "No more than a baby witch."

The witch raised her hand and slashed down in an arc of green lightning, throwing a spell over Jean-Luc and Sabine, burning his retinas and searing.

Chapter 32

SABINE

Brilliant green light enveloped Sabine and Thibodeaux as Georgette's spell hit.

Sabine couldn't see past the flares in her vision. Throwing her hands out, her fingers interlaced with the electrical pulses, singeing her fingers. She clutched her hands into fists and yanked. A primal groan sounded from beyond the light.

Georgette held tight to her spell, but Sabine jerked. Once she had loot in her grasp, she didn't let go. Once she touched it, it was hers. No one was a better thief than she.

The flare of the witch's spell faded. Sabine blinked away the ghosted image of lightning. When her vision cleared, only she and Thibodeaux remained in the midst of the overblown sculptures.

Masked figures in flowing robes climbed the ladder and filed down the sides of the float. Each carried crates full of beads and other trinkets. Others followed with bottles of champagne and plastic flutes. The krewe members gave them curious looks as they passed. While Sabine tried to get her bearings, the floats' engines roared to life, and the platform jolted as it started to roll forward. Krewe set down their crates and clasped the railing, chattering and strategizing over the best techniques for throwing beads.

One of the masked, robed figures stopped to address them. "You," he pointed at Thibodeaux. "Either hop off or pull on your tunic and mask. You, too." He gestured to Sabine. She nodded and made a show of putting on her mask while Thibodeaux flashed that badge of his. The krewe member grunted in response, put on his own mask, and headed to the front of the float.

The rage coloring Thibodeaux's face subsided, replaced by astonishment.

"You stopped it," he said. Under different circumstances, Sabine would've been offended at the incredulity in his voice.

"The Iceman and witch vanished," she said. "And I can't see Oliver or Meg. How long do you think we have to get them out?"

"If they're doing this for sport, I figure they'll want to put on a show. So, I'm guessing the clock runs out when we hit Canal Street. Maybe two hours. Maybe."

"Unless they just trigger it now," Sabine hissed.

Thibodeaux looked more himself. Calculating. "I don't think they will. This is a game for them."

"That tracks with Meg's memory of them. So, maybe two hours. We find those two pieces of sh—"

"First, we get Meg and Oliver out. Those two aren't going anywhere while the float's moving."

"Agreed," Sabine conceded. Thibodeaux was thinking clearer than her now. "So, how do we do that?"

"How did you stop that spell the witch threw at us?"

"I stole it." Sabine held out her hand, uncurling her fingers to reveal a sparking green orb. She felt the smug smile stretching her cheeks despite their desperate situation.

"Do you know how the spell works?" His eyes were appraising now. Not like the snarling beast from a moment ago. When this was over, she had to learn more about that black crap in his eyes and how to get rid of it.

"I'm guessing it's a containment spell. She was trying to trap us, too. The air sparked with the same lightning when you reappeared. And it feels like the spell on the door at that guy's apartment, you know, from before," Sabine finished awkwardly.

"Can you steal the one holding Meg and Oliver?"

"I . . . Maybe? I've only done it by accident, catching them while Georgette threw them around." She sounded so stupid and inept, but Thibodeaux looked at her encouragingly. He gave her that smile that flustered her.

"I'll try," she said, stuffing the spell under her toga and into her satchel.

"If we can get them out before this float hits the parade route, we could save lives," Thibodeaux said.

No pressure there.

Staggering to the edge of the float, Sabine stumbled as it went from the parking lot to the street, getting in line for the parade. Thibodeaux caught her around the waist and held on until she steadied herself. She tried to give him a thank you smile back, but it felt awkward and strained, and he let go.

Wedging herself between two of the toga-clad krewe members, she held onto the railing with one hand and reached out with the other, raking her fingers through the air.

The guy to her left laughed down at her. "Practicing your bead throwing technique?"

She bared her teeth at him in a semblance of a smile as she felt the edge of the spell field and sparks lit around her fingers.

"Cool," the guy said. The bourbon on his breath reached her past his mask and into hers. She coughed it back out.

You can do this. You are a master thief. Just take it.

Sabine clenched her fist and yanked. It pulled inward in a blazing green sheet. Crouching, she pulled harder. It fought her.

A familiar arm wound around her waist. Together, she and Thibodeaux hauled the spell inward. The krewe to either side gaped. The green lightning reflected in their eyes.

Then it jerked from her grasp and snapped back into place. Sabine fell against Thibodeaux. Her slight weight, along with the pothole the float hit, brought them both down. He sat hard and caught her in his lap, holding her a moment too long.

Instinctively, she wrestled out of his hold, despite how safe it felt to be there. She bounced to her feet and went back in to try again.

Thibodeaux laid a hand on her shoulder and leaned in.

"It's too big." *And you're too weak*. He didn't need to say it for it to be true.

"I've got an idea," he said, letting go.

The float lurched back and forth as it rumbled down the uneven street. The gathered crowds lining the sidewalks screamed, and the krewe answered, throwing trinkets. Streams of beads flew. The shouts grew wilder. Hands waved, snatching the shiny plastic treasures from the air. Bacchus Parade had begun.

Time was running out.

Thibodeaux set his legs apart in a firing stance to keep his balance. Sabine wavered, and his strong fingers wrapped around her arms. She fought the urge to shrug them off as he brought his face to hers. His warm breath brushed her ear as he spoke close enough for her to hear.

"If I can get you inside, take the clock from around Oliver's neck. It's the countdown. Meg doesn't have one. If you can see them, aim for him."

"What are you going to do?" she asked, not knowing if he could hear her.

"If the lightning is holding them in. Then the mists must be keeping them from view." She could barely hear him over the blood pounding in her ears. "Keeping you from seeing them. And maybe from touching them."

"Don't," she whispered, guessing what he planned.

Thibodeaux let go of her. He would do it. He had people to save, and he wouldn't stop until his job was done. He gave her an encouraging nod, then his face turned hard.

It frightened Sabine to see him like that.

Tendrils crawled across his eyes until they were fully black, and he stepped away from her.

Sabine reached for him, but he was gone.

Chapter 33

THIBODEAUX

The darkness came easily.

Too easily.

Jean-Luc stepped into it. He could not fight with magic. Not until now. It writhed within him, and the mists called to it. Warwick had said it was dark magic. Better left untouched.

"Come on," he spoke to the darkness. "You work with me, and we'll have a reckoning afterwards."

Talking to dark magic, probably not a good sign. But he was out of good options. He'd settle for those he had. Jean-Luc was not going to lose another person on his watch. He'd tried to do it the right way.

Now he'd do it the other way.

His jaw ached as he ground his teeth, attempting to pull at the darkness as Sabine had pulled at the containment spell. He reached for it as the float rolled along the parade route, ticking down the minutes. He repositioned himself in a fighter's stance and pulled again.

It resisted him.

The rage built, roiling in his gut.

These creatures came to his world and threw around their magic, and he couldn't do a damned thing about it.

How dare they!

There it was. The darkness whispered to him. And he felt a smile creep across his face.

"That's it. You know you want me. Come and take me."

It should have frightened Jean-Luc at how easily the darkness answered him now. The sorrow on Sabine's face should have worried him, but the familiarity of the black mists welcoming him held the whole of his attention. He had no room for petty feelings, such as loss or fear. No concerns reached him here. He was part of the darkness. He should have seen it before. Saved himself from the torment of pushing it away.

The two humans he'd come for cowered under the god's legs, staring up at him. They, too, were frightened. It felt good. It felt right.

Jean-Luc held out his arms in a parody of the Eros statue. He thought he heard it laugh at him. The mists swirled around his arms. It no longer fought him.

It flowed from the corners of the float, coalescing around him. He threw his head back and breathed it in. It coursed down his throat and into his lungs. It ran through his arteries, down his nerves, filling him with power and sensation.

The air cleared so that Sabine could see him. A god himself. No longer weak and trapped. He flexed his arms to show her the power he had taken in, but she cowered away. Unease coiled in his gut at the look on her face, but the rising tide of darkness quickly overshadowed it.

Heads turned, first a couple, then more. One krewe member tapped another until the full fleet of masked figures looked upon him, afraid. As if he were their god rather than Eros.

Jean-Luc threw back his head and laughed at the float's fake god. A real one has arrived.

Chapter 34

<hr>

SABINE

Thibodeau hovered over her. His face drawn and nasty. Black veins spider webbed across his cheeks and up his temples. His hands were curled and clawlike.

Sabine fell back behind the statue of the sprawling couple. Afraid of him—something she hadn't thought was possible. Then the two figures under the God statue caught her attention.

Meg and Oliver's faces mirrored the feeling she had. That brought Sabine to her senses. She promised to do a job. She would save Thibodeau later.

If she could.

Crawling around the feet of the happy, carved couple, she snuck up behind Oliver. Meg saw her. Sabine motioned with a finger pressed to her lips for her to remain quiet. Meg gave an almost imperceptible nod and drew Oliver close. Sabine brushed his hair away from his eyes. He looked up at her, confused.

"Are you okay?" she asked in a calm voice that belied the emotions raging through her.

Without waiting for an answer. She ran her fingers through his hair and down his neck. Her fingertips found the chain's latch. In an instant, she snapped it open and snatched the necklace. He cried out as she took it triumphantly.

Relief washed over his face. His eyes rolled up in his head, and the lids closed over them. Meg hugged him to her chest as Sabine checked his pulse.

"He's okay," she said. "Just passed out."

"I don't blame him," Meg said. "Can you get us out?"

"I know someone who can," Sabine said, rising to her feet, ready to go on the hunt for Georgette. She slipped the watch into her pocket and immediately felt its rhythm sink with her heart.

"Oh Shit!"

"What is it?" Meg asked. "Are you okay, Sabine?"

"I don't think so," Sabine said as she hit her knees.

Chapter 35

THIBODEAUX

J ean-Luc looked down at the trio.

Sabine lay dying.

He hadn't calculated that stealing the timepiece would sync it with her heart. He should've known. With him, the timepiece had only been borrowed.

Sabine was a thief. If she stole it, that made it hers.

Mlle. Georgette would answer for this.

Jean-Luc threw statues aside, hunting for the witch. One crashed into the railing. Its head cracked off and rolled into the street. Tourists dodged either side to evade the disembodied head.

Krewe members dove at Jean-Luc, trying to stop his rampage. But no one could stop him. He grabbed the first to reach him and ripped off their mask, throwing it like a trinket into the crowd. Not knowing any better, the people cheered and fought to catch it.

The person in his grasp was not Georgette. Jean-Luc shoved her aside and grabbed another krewe member, ripping their mask off. Not Georgette. He threw the man down. He repeated with each person coming at him until they stopped coming. Then he went back to overturning statues, knowing that cowardly witch hid behind one of them.

The next carved figure cracked in half at the waist and fell into the street, knocking one of the pedestrians to the ground. But he did not stop. He would not stop until he had the witch in his hands.

Chapter 36

WARWICK

Warwick stepped out of his glamour, coughing and spluttering. He could hold on no longer. Thibodeau had drunk in the dark magic like an elixir. But not before it corroded Warwick's throat.

Even a goblin can only hold their breath for so long.

He'd watched the humans fighting so hard to save one another. Where goblins usually chose to go after one another's throat. It had been what turned him from his people. Left him to live a solitary life. Caused him to believe that people don't truly care.

All those had been excuses that allowed him to sell trinkets holding dark magic. And giving the humans faelight earrings or charm bracelets to capture the memories was not enough to make up for the tragedy he had enabled. Warwick could see that so plainly playing out on this weird edifice to a god that was only a fable to these people.

Thibodeaux hunted until he found the witch. His hands closed around her throat. This was not the man Warwick had met. This was a man being eaten alive by dark magic. Magic that Warwick had allowed to enter this world.

On hands and knees, Sabine gasped for air and struggled to keep the ticking of her heart from falling into rhythm with the timepiece.

A single spark of hope came to him.

Warwick went to the fledgling witch first. The young man next to her was unconscious, and no concern of his. The tall woman, too far past horror to be surprised by a goblin at her side, now cradled Sabine in her arms.

Cupping Sabine's hand, which grasped the timepiece, Warwick whispered into her ear. "This charm was not set to your heart. You stole it. It does not belong to you. You are a thief. Let it go."

But she didn't.

Her eyes rolled to meet his. Her mouth struck a hard line. This witch had more power than he had seen before. He had been blind. Or she was clever enough to hide it.

Sabine snatched the timepiece from her neck. Warwick held out his hand to take it. But she threw it from the float.

"Pity the soul that catches it. They shall not be as strong as you," Warwick said, nearly feeling a pang of sorrow for the unknown stranger.

When Sabine heard his words, she launched to her feet and reached out as if she could bring it back. Though she might be powerful, she did not yet know how to use her power.

The necklace sailed through the air just as the fake human jewels had moments before. An unsuspecting human jumped and caught it. Since it was the only item now thrown from Eros's float, the triumphant human was shoved aside by the crowd, trying to claim the cursed item as their own. The man fumbled it, and the timepiece rolled into the street.

The cart rolled past, crushing it under a wheel.

Murky magic bloomed around the float, knocking out all of Eros's devotees. At once, they went from cowering along the railing to crumpled forms at the bottom of the cart. And strangely, the toga on Eros's statue fluttered in the breeze.

A male emerged from the carved form. Baylur stepped out of the glamour which had merged him with the god statue. His choice to meld with this particular god was perverse. Baylur was a creature of desire only, no love to temper it. And Warwick had enabled him.

The goblin crouched down behind the coupling statue, like the coward that he was, and watched. As Sabine stepped gently over the prone bodies of the Eros's pretend worshipers, making her way toward Detective Thibodeaux, who held Georgette in a death grip.

Meanwhile, Baylur beckoned to Megan Armand.

The tall one went to the Fae and leaned in as he wrapped an arm around her and held out a hand. She looked to him as if she didn't understand. The Fae bared his sharp teeth and squinted his eyes. Warwick knew the Fae was irritated at her hesitation. He had pursued her, and she had evaded him longer than any other.

Baylur would have her for his pride alone. He would also wish to show Mlle. Georgette that none refused him. Megan was the one needle that the heartless witch could use to prick him.

To Warwick's dismay, but not his surprise, Megan reached for her chest.

Now is the time for bravery, he told himself. You are of the Great Goblin Court. If you ever wish to be accepted back, you will begin by showing this bit of boldness. If not this, then you deserve your banishment from the court as well as from the Beyond.

Rising behind Megan, he pressed the moon charm into the nape of her neck with his thumb. At first, nothing changed. She clawed at her chest, raising whelps. But her hand slowed and stopped. She clasped it to the back of her neck, catching the charm as Warwick let go and stepped to the side.

Megan held it to her skin as her brow wrinkled, then she brought it around and held it out in her palm to show Baylur. His teeth flashed in anger.

Faster than a human could perceive, the Fae bent to rip out her neck with his teeth.

Faster than a human, but not faster than Warwick. He shoved Megan Armand aside, and they both tumbled under the god's legs, tangling together.

Megan beat at Warwick, perhaps thinking he was the Fae. But, while they tumbled, Baylur had disappeared. Warwick lay still, accepting the blows until her fists stilled, then stopped.

"I am sorry," Megan said. Tears fell from her eyes onto his cheeks. He believed her emotions stemmed from actions long since passed. Memories lost before this night.

The goblin sat up and wiped the tears from her cheeks with the cuff of his coat. "It is I who am sorry."

And, perhaps for the first time in his life, he was.

Chapter 37

SABINE

Assuring herself that the cursed timepiece had shattered under the wheels of the float, Sabine checked the fallen bodies. The Krewe of Eros still breathed. Hearts still beat. The shock wave of the powerful magic had thrown them into a stupor. Which gave her time to search for Georgette.

Only to find that Thibodeaux had her by the throat.

"Jean-Luc! No!" she called to him as she ran forward on the float, which had finally come to a halt, backing up the parade. Either he didn't hear her or he was beyond listening. She could not let him kill this woman, no matter how terrible she might be. It would mean the end of the person that Thibodeaux used to be. Still *was* inside, she corrected herself.

Reaching under her costume toga, Sabine dug in her satchel and pulled out a spell. It was bright blue. She didn't know what the colors meant and didn't have time to figure out.

"Good enough," she said and threw it.

It hit Thibodeaux and the witch. Their feet left the platform as they rose into the air about two feet, maybe more. Thibodeaux did not loosen his hold. Georgette's feet kicked frantically beneath her.

"Not good."

She reached and threw another. A flock of shadow crows circled the float screeching. Georgette still hung from the detective's grasp, her face turning a disturbing shade of crimson.

"That's it. You're getting them all."

Sabine lobbed spell after spell without waiting to see which hit and which missed, or what they did once they found their mark. Her hand landed on a buzzing spell at the bottom and a smile inched across her face.

"Here we go!"

She threw the black, writhing mass at them. It struck and erupted into a swarm of wasps. They swirled around the pair in a vortex, hiding them from view. Sabine only had two orbs left. With one in each hand, she aimed carefully, but stopped just short of throwing.

The vortex of wasps collapsed in on the detective and the witch and began stinging them. Thibodeaux dropped the witch, who fell to the platform, coughing and spluttering. She waved, and the wasps dissipated into thin air as Thibodeaux landed on the float beside her.

Sabine shoved the last two spells back into her satchel and ran to the front, stopping between the two, her hands held out to keep them apart. She feared Thibodeaux in this state might go for her throat, but she could not give up hope that the man she knew was in there somewhere. And that man would not harm her.

Blue lights flashed below and police swarmed up the ladder, hands on holsters. The crowd had been pushed back away from the float.

Thibodeaux's black eyes landed on Sabine. She felt the darkness looking at her through him. Hungry.

"Thibodeaux, back away."

He held his ground.

"Jean-Luc," she pleaded as officers made their way to the front of the float.

His body convulsed. Thibodeaux blinked, and his eyes cleared. Though a haze remained, she could see his gold flecked irises. His pupils grew wide in the dim light.

"Sabine?"

She tried for a cocky smile. "Of the Domingue Witches."

An officer stopped at Thibodeaux's side. Two more behind Georgette.

"Sir, what happened here?"

Thibodeaux cleared his throat as he looked around at the damage he had done. He squeezed his eyes shut, then the official mask of the New Orleans's detective lowered over his face.

"Check on the krewe members. You will find a young man, first name, Oliver, behind the main statue. He needs immediate medical attention. Arrest Mlle. Georgette for his attempted murder. You will also need to arrest—" He looked around.

Sabine suspected he was looking for the Fae and shook her head. There would be no finding him and no keeping him if they did. Thibodeaux gave a minute nod.

"That's it for now. Hop to it."

Sabine slumped onto the outstretched arm of the overturned statue of a young Greek male reaching out to his lover. She tried to give Thibodeaux an encouraging smile, but they both knew this would not end well for him.

His eyes strayed to below her neck where the timepiece had rested as it fought to sync with her heart. Thibodeaux shook his head, his eyes filled with shame. He had fought Georgette while Sabine lay dying.

She didn't blame him. He had not been himself.

Sabine tried to offer a comforting smile and failed.

Chapter 38

THIBODEAUX

Sunday, in the early morning hours, the guards at Central Lockup greeted Jean-Luc with restrained pleasantries. Rumors of the parade's chaos had already filtered in. Expecting to be relieved of his position, he'd brought his sidearm and badge, expecting to leave with neither. He only had a short window to implement his plan.

An officer escorted him into a corridor lined with holding cells. He'd come for Mlle. Georgette.

They probably wouldn't be able to hold the witch past Monday. Not without matching DNA evidence from the fingernails found lodged in the streetcar victim's chest. But DNA evidence took a while to process. And might not be enough to put her away. It would not help Tyler Davis, who Jean-Luc suspected was also her victim. Maybe her first. Maybe there were hundreds, but not in his town.

He had this morning before rumors started turning into official records.

The officer asked, "Should I set up an interrogation room, sir?"

"No, I just need to verify that she is here. You can go on back. I'll only be a minute."

This was not proper protocol, and they both knew it, but Jean-Luc had earned some clout in his years on the force. He was cashing it all in this morning. The officer shifted uncomfortably. His hand twitched towards his radio. Then he shrugged.

"All right, sir. I can give you a few minutes."

"I won't be long," Jean-Luc assured him.

The man hurried down the corridor, not wanting to be party to what came next. Once he closed the door and was out of sight, Jean-Luc proceeded down the row, glancing in windows. He knew which one he was looking for, but he was stalling.

Before he reached Georgette's cell, a diminutive figure appeared at the far end of the corridor, coming out of what must be an empty cell. Sabine's slippered feet were silent on the linoleum floor.

"Should I ask how you got in?"

"No, you should not," she answered and held out her hand. "You got it?"

He slipped a wristwatch that he had *liberated* from the evidence room into her hand. Sabine had specifically asked for the pocket watch that had held him captive in the apartment last fall, but he denied keeping it. He suspected she knew he was lying, but he couldn't seem to part with it.

The spherical timepiece from last night had been shattered beneath the parade float. Since Warwick couldn't get back into the Beyond to procure another one, the remaining available enchanted watch had come from the streetcar victim.

"All right, let's get this over with. We don't have much time." Jean-Luc stood to the side as Sabine crouched in front of the designated cell and went to work on the lock. When she suggested this scheme, probably to ward off another attempt by him to strangle the witch, he hadn't believed she could do it, but she'd made it this far past guards and security cameras.

"Will the cameras pick you up?" he asked again.

"I told you no." She sighed. "I borrowed a spell from Warwick to hide me."

"You *borrowed* it."

"*Yes*. You want to sit and chat about my means and methods, or do you want to get this done?"

Jean-Luc twirled his hand to indicate for her to get a move on.

When the door eased open, he shifted his body to block it from the camera as she slipped inside. She was there only a minute before cracking the door and whispering. "Your turn."

With his back still to the opening, he took a deep breath and pushed. Jean-Luc had practiced through the night. The rage swelled. He clamped down on it and funneled the black mists out of his hands. Holding them behind his back, He aimed the darkness through the opening while Sabine slipped out.

"Okay," he said when he was done.

"You emptied all of it out?" Sabine asked.

"Yeah," he lied. "Back to you."

Sabine pulled a green sparking ball from her satchel and ran it along the door to the cell to set the containment spell in place. She stood back to examine her work, then ducked back inside.

He caught her arm. "How long will it take?"

"When are they likely to check on her?"

"First shift, a couple of hours from now, if I work it right."

"Then work it right," Sabine said. "That should be enough time. I don't think it will take long to break her."

"And if it does?"

"If she doesn't agree, I leave the witch, and she watches the clock tick down in the dark, alone, and unseen until her heart explodes."

"Sounds like a plan," Jean-Luc said.

Sabine laughed. "You're ruthless."

He did not laugh back.

"Thibodeaux."

"Yeah?"

"Thanks."

"For?"

"Cleaning up my aunt's place."

"Who says I did?"

"Some stupid birdie told me," Sabine said and disappeared inside to give the witch an ultimatum.

As he left, Jean-Luc nodded at the officer that let him in. The man gave a half smile in return.

As Jean-Luc exited the building, Carmichael came storming in from the parking lot. Upon seeing the detective, she turned to follow him back outside. Either the officer, or one of the guards, must have notified her that he'd come in to confront the witch. Carmichael had probably left instructions for them to call if he showed up.

She gave him a flat look. "If I go in there, what will I find?"

"I would leave it until morning. Then you should find a healthy, if shaken, Mlle. Georgette ready to confess to murder."

"Did you touch her?" Carmichael asked.

"Not this morning."

"What did you do?"

"Just looked in to see that she was locked up tight. Didn't enter the cell or speak to her if that's what you're worried about.

If you play your cards right, this could be your first and maybe highest profile case, cracked with no effort on your part. Unless you count suppressing evidence."

"What do you mean by that?" Her eyes shifted and her throat bobbed.

"Have a good day." Jean-Luc walked away.

"I'll let her sit until noon. But we're going to talk back at the office," she·called after him.

Jean-Luc waved and got into his car, knowing he'd already be gone before Carmichael arrived at headquarters. He'd already tidied up his files and unlocked his computer password. Next, he'd drop off his gun and badge, then head home to figure out how to keep this city safe against forces they didn't even know existed.

But that was for tomorrow.

Today, he'd get some sleep, knowing one murderer was off the streets.

Chapter 39

SABINE

The French Market teemed with tourists. Sabine and Meg wove their way amongst the people like real New Orleaners. Well, maybe real natives of the city wouldn't be sprinkled in powdered sugar as they licked beignet crumbs off their sticky fingers.

Bertrand the Blasted Crow perched on the canopy, keeping a beady eye on them, and the grumbly goblin followed in their wake. Meg kept up a streaming commentary on the wares displayed in the open-air pavilion. After cleaning her fingers, Sabine let her hands swing loosely at her sides, gathering bits and baubles from passing strangers to stow in the many pockets of her auburn jumper.

The four of them had agreed to come and survey the market for any lasting effects of the Black Goo. None of her three companions had agreed to the nickname, but seeing that none of them had offered a better one, in her estimation, it remained the Black Goo.

Warwick had taken up residence in the tiny wooden potting shed in her aunt's backyard, or rather, Sabine's backyard. She had to keep reminding herself that she was now a legit homeowner. A fact which she conveniently forgot anytime Meg had a complaint about the plumbing.

Sabine suspected Warwick only agreed to join them at the market in order to assure himself no rift in the Greater Goblin Continuum had opened since the night he came with the detective. This name had also been her contribution, because the other three were sorely lacking in creativity.

Instead of being useful and assisting in the naming of things and places and people, they insisted on asking about Thibodeaux and rules and laws. None of which Sabine was interested in discussing.

"So, Georgette feels so remorseful she just confesses to multiple crimes?" Meg asked, attempting and failing to brush sugar from her plush blue sweater. "Doesn't sound like her at all."

"I had a little talk with her," Sabine said, stashing a liberated onyx necklace into her satchel.

"And she admitted to dating men just to snatch their hearts?" Meg shuddered.

"She and your Fae—"

"He's not mine," Meg cut her off, rubbing a hand self-consciously across her chest. "He didn't want me. He just wanted me to tear out my heart for him."

"So, just your basic abusive boyfriend."

"No. Yeah. I guess. But he wanted it literally." Meg closed her eyes tight enough to cause premature crow's feet. Sabine's chest ached at the thought of how close Meg had come to snatching out her own heart for that fucked up Fae.

"But you said no."

"Only because I didn't have one to give him."

"He'll be back now that she does," Warwick muttered. Sabine gave him a sharp look, but Meg didn't seem to hear him. He raised his eyebrows as if to say, she needs to know.

Meg pulled Sabine to a halt. "Here, try this on." Her overly tall roommate held a silver satyr mask up to Sabine's face. "You never know when you might have to cosplay as a creature."

"I'm assuming most creatures are not shiny and bedazzled," Sabine said, putting the bejeweled mask back on the rack, much to the vendor's disappointment.

Meg looked to Warwick for confirmation.

The goblin shrugged. "Some do tend toward the flashy side."

"Really?" Meg asked, fascinated by this bit of trivia. Sabine was relieved at the change of subject. Then Meg's attention snapped back to her inquisition.

"So, Georgette and Baylur. They're just playing Hot Potato with hearts?"

"You feeling hungry? I'll pay." Sabine said as they passed a hoagie stand. It was a little joke of hers. She never paid.

"You just stuffed your face with fried dough. You're not hungry. You're trying to distract me," Meg accused her but stopped and looked the menu over, anyway. "We'll come back after we check out the Middle." Meg's nickname for the blasted area of the market. Not very inventive. "You were explaining the game."

Sabine lifted her eyebrows as if confused.

"If you'd rather not discuss Georgette, you could tell me what's up with you and Thibodeaux."

"Witch," Sabine grumbled.

"Back at you. Now, spill it. You and Thibodeaux trapped Georgette, strapped a timepiece on her, and she spills all the gory details?"

"Including a view of that gaping hole in her chest where her heart presumably used to hang out." Sabine shuddered. "How does no one else notice that her corset is always damp with blood, or entrail juices, or—"

"Focus." Meg glowered down from her mighty height. "Georgette. Baylur. Why do they do it? How do they do it?"

"Magic." Sabine kept walking, but Meg caught her ponytail and dragged her to a stop.

"Fine." Sabine jerked her hair loose of Meg's grip. "You know Baylur."

Meg grunted.

"He did his thing on Georgette." Sabine waggled her fingers to indicate the unnerving allure of the Fae. "He deserts her. She begs for him to come back. He asks for her heart. She says yes. He says, 'Literally, I want your heart.' So, she rips open her own chest and hands it to him. That piece of Fae trash."

Taking a breath to resume her gory tale, Sabine realized she'd left her housemate behind. Warwick stood just behind and to the left as if prepared to catch Meg, half again as tall as him. He cut his eyes to Sabine.

What? She asked me to tell her. Sabine defended herself silently.

Craaw. Craaw, the crow reprimanded her loudly. She searched for him to thump his feathered head, but he perched out of reach on a rack of hats near Meg.

Sabine went back and stood beside her, facing the same direction and close enough that their elbows almost touched.

"You wouldn't have given it to him."

"I gave it to Valdi."

"First of all, that is totally different. Second of all, you didn't literally break open your ribcage and hand it over."

Cr-r-r-uck.

"I might have." Meg's shoulders slumped.

Not knowing how to help, Sabine relieved a shopper of the cookie that was almost certainly going to fall out of her bag of baked goods and handed it to Meg. Her shoulders lifted and fell with a heavy sigh as she took a bite.

"There, that's better," Sabine announced, hoping that it was.

"Go on. I'm fortified with sugar. I can handle it."

Warwick muttered and Bertrand made disagreeable tocking sounds, but Sabine did as she was told. This once.

"Baylur didn't care. He just wanted to see if she'd do it. Who knows what he did with the heart once he had it? But Georgette couldn't be shaken loose. She knew how to get into the Beyond on her own." Sabine checked on Warwick. He didn't seem to be paying attention to the conversation as they threaded through the vendors' tables. But she knew he was there to look for his own way back to the Beyond.

"Eventually, Georgette soothed her hurt feelings by charming this hipster dude, Tyler Davis. Which ticked off that Fae prig. He didn't like being replaced. So he decides on a new game. He tells Georgette he'll give her her heart back if she can convince this Tyler fellow to give her his. But Baylur attached strings to the deal."

"Of course he did. He is Fae," Warwick added. So, he was listening.

"Got that right," Sabine said. "Georgette had to get the heart before this cursed timepiece winds down or his heart explodes."

Meg shuddered and stuffed the rest of the cookie in her mouth to ward off evil.

"Georgette traps Tyler in his apartment so he doesn't wander off. Baylur adds a little dark magic to disappear the guy. Tyler's time runs out. His heart explodes. But Baylur is a good sport. He helps a witch out by glamouring his body to look like that of a recently lost woman."

"Valdi," Meg said with more conviction and less sorrow than Sabine would have expected.

"Round Two. Streetcar guy. Georgette kept him trapped in a crypt in the cemetery. It didn't look like he was going to hand over his heart, either. She gets mad and, just before the time runs out, she rips it out for him. Baylur says that doesn't count and refuses to cover up this murder for her.

"She's pissed off now and reckless. She just wants Baylur's attention however she can get it. So, she stages the guy's body on the Canal streetcar and stows his heart in her chest where it rots. Baylur is not impressed. He's off trying to steal another heart."

They all pause, pretending to admire an artist's paintings while Meg composed herself. With no cookies at hand, Sabine didn't know what to do. A group of chatty teens bumped into Meg's shoulder but veered around Warwick without seeming to actually see him.

Crocka, Bertrand said comfortingly, and they moved on.

"And Oliver? Did she really like him?" Meg asked as she picked up a cerulean blue silk scarf, tried it on, checked the price tag, and put it back.

As they moved on, Sabine retrieved the scarf and tucked it into her satchel. Meg's birthday was coming up in a month and she'd need a present.

"Oliver. This is my theory. I couldn't get her to confirm it. But I think Georgette was beginning to like this game. It annoyed Baylur when she had a new boy toy. He'd come back around to give her attention as they played another round of Will-He/Won't-He Snatch His Heart Out?"

"I'd buy that version," Meg said as they approached the blast zone near the center of the market.

Warwick grunted in agreement.

Creeeek, Bertrand confirmed.

Odd to have all four of them agree on anything. But Sabine was pleased. It was her idea, after all. And who better to theorize on stealing, hearts or otherwise, than her?

In the affected area, the Black Goo had all dissipated, and the market roof had been patched. All seemed normal at first. But the vendors' wares gradually shifted from fanciful masks, colorful silk wraps, and sparkling jewelry to sneering demon faces carved in wood, capes so black they drank in the sunlight, and gems that pulsed with darkness.

Warwick skirted around the perimeter of these darker booths. Sabine fell into step behind him while Meg wandered, clueless, through the middle.

"Meg," Sabine hissed. Her housemate searched for the two of them as if she couldn't see them past the dark booths.

Bertrand croaked to get her attention and strafed Meg on his way to Sabine and the goblin.

"Oh." Meg's eyes grew round as she realized the others had left her. She backed out of the booths to join them.

Vendors' eyes followed her hungrily.

"Maybe we should stick together."

"You think?" Sabine said, taking ahold of her arm and guiding her out from under the pavilion roof to the sunlight. Warwick stopped at the edge, remaining in the shadows. He stood so that he could keep an eye on the market's interior, lest something sneak up on him, Sabine thought.

"You don't think any of it's cursed, do you?" Meg looked over the goblin's head toward the offending booths.

"I don't think we need to test it. Do you?" Sabine asked.

Bertrand cawed in agreement.

Meg looked crestfallen, which Sabine found odd. Wasn't she at least a little leery after her time in the Beyond?

Warwick studied Meg's expression, and Sabine caught his eye.

He shook his head. "It's not over. Not yet."

Author's Note

New Orleans drew me back twice this winter, luring me in with its stories of the Voodoo bone lady, society tombs, and Zelda with her trifflin' children. It trapped my imagination behind shifting walls of crumbling brick and freshly painted wrought iron. There I found two crows atop a crypt in St. Louis No.1, croaking out their judgment at the likes of us living inhabiting the city of the dead.

The dark alleys whispered secrets as jazz bands wailed from clubs, their French doors thrown open to the night, their neon beckoning me inside. Remnants of this year's Mardi Gras parade hung from trees and balconies, colorful strings of plastic beads glistening in the sun. These visits provided the perfect re-immersion into the Big Easy with all its stories built up over centuries. Just what I needed as I edit Book Three, *A Clever Fox*.

But now that I'm safely home, I need to catch up with my fellow book-loving friends and family who share my obsession. Holly who grew up with me, passing books back and forth on the school bus since 5th grade. Alana and Annette who assure me that they love me but would probably love me more if I slipped them a new book soon. And Rob who tucks me in at night with a glass of wine and an abundance of books on the bedside table.

Thank you, dear readers, for joining me in New Orleans with all its hidden mysteries and magic. Meet you there again this summer.

About the Author

Julia V. Ashley writes contemporary fantasy, paranormal mysteries, and the occasional peculiar tale, including *Jazz by Faelight: Original Short Stories of Hidden Magic in the Big Easy* and "No Nibbling on the Neighbors," a short story in the anthology *Vampire Survival Guide*. As an architect, Julia finds inspiration delving into the crumbling buildings of the Gothic South where she grew up. She lives along the Natchez Trace Parkway with her husband, a dog-like creature who makes for a dubious familiar, and a varied wildlife roaming the woods.

Connect with Julia

https://juliavashley.com

Join THE DREAMARC newsletter for a free prequel story.

https://subscribepage.io/JuliaVAshley-Newsletter